Insatiable

A HORROR ROMANCE

THE PRIMAL SINS COLLECTION
BOOK ONE

SEPHYRRA
CORDELIA MIRE

WITHER & RUNE PRESS

To all the women over 35, plus-size, and absolutely fabulous. This one's for you. For those who know their worth, embrace their curves, and dive headfirst into the world of monster romance. And to everyone who's watched a horror film and thought the chase was just a bit too sexy—this is especially for you. After all, why settle for ordinary when a monster love story is so much more fun?

Content Advisory

This is the expanded edition of *Insatiable*, originally published as a novella. This version contains new chapters, extended scenes, and additional character development.

Insatiable is a horror romance that explores obsession, desire, and psychological darkness. It includes violence, physical abuse, emotional manipulation, infidelity, explicit sexual content, lactation kink as a central theme, dubious consent, pregnancy loss, body image struggles, substance use, and supernatural power imbalance.

If any of these topics fall outside your comfort zone, this may not be the right read for you. Your boundaries matter — please honor them.

Chapter One

I jolted awake with my chest aching hard enough to make me gasp. I pressed a hand to my breasts. They were full and heavy, straining against my pajama top like grief had settled there. A groan slipped out before I could stop it. The clock on my nightstand glowed a dull green, 4:17 a.m. Again.

"Men couldn't handle this for a day," I muttered, kicking the damp sheets off my legs. Sweat had pasted my pajamas to every curve, every fold of skin, turning the cotton into a heat that bordered on suffocating. The ceiling stared back at me, water-stained, unfamiliar, not mine. None of this was mine.

The ache came every night. Some nights it closed around me, a slow grip behind the sternum. Other nights it sat heavy, a dull pressure that spread from my chest into my ribs, my throat, the backs of my teeth. Tonight it lingered somewhere between the two, persistent, almost cruel in its patience. I tried to breathe through it the way the nurses had shown me, slow inhales counted to four, but my body had stopped cooperating with my mind months ago. The pressure kept building, and I knew, the way you know a storm is coming before the thunder, that I had no choice but to give in.

I sighed and sat up. The apartment swallowed the sound whole.

The only noise was the low rattle of the old fridge in the kitchen and the distant wash of cars on the road below. Just enough to remind me I wasn't sealed inside a tomb. Just enough to make the silence worse. I hated living alone. I wasn't built for it. Growing up in the South, in a house that always felt too small for how many people were crammed inside, there was never a quiet moment. Cousins draped across the couch fighting over the remote, siblings shouting through thin walls, and Mama's voice cutting through all of it, *Set the table, I'm not asking again.* We weren't rich. We weren't even comfortable most months. But my parents made sure that house was full, full of noise in a way no amount of money could manufacture.

Now it was just me. This apartment didn't feel like mine. It was rented and cold, like I was squatting in someone else's half-finished life, waiting for a direction that never came. If Mama knew I was living in the city alone, she'd clutch her chest and go full *Oh Lord, have mercy.* I hadn't told her much. I couldn't. She'd been so happy at the wedding. I didn't have the stomach to shatter that memory. So none of my family knew the truth. None of them knew the whole of it. The worst parts stayed locked in me.

I rubbed my temples and reached for the lamp, flicking it on. Pale yellow light spilled across the nightstand, catching the breast pump right where I'd left it, cap still off from last night's session. I picked it up. The plastic was cool in my hands. Something I barely registered anymore. It was just part of the routine, like brushing my teeth, like pretending to sleep. I set it up without thinking, attached it, and turned it on. The first pull was sharp, a sharp sting that made me wince and clench the sheet in my fist. But I knew it would ease in a few minutes. It always did.

The heartache stayed. It lodged behind my sternum like a bone that had healed wrong.

I lay back and closed my eyes, letting the machine do its work. The rhythmic hum filled the dark room, a mechanical lullaby for no one.

I'd bought this pump when I was still pregnant. Still hopeful. Still stupid enough to believe the nursery I'd painted seafoam green would actually hold a baby. I'd pictured myself in the rocking chair I found at the thrift store, feeding my child, singing something soft and tuneless. I had dreams — dreams I should have known better than to trust — where everything turned out fine. Where the man I married would stand in the doorway and tell me we were going to be okay.

But those dreams didn't survive.

And the baby didn't either.

I didn't let myself go further than that. Not now, not at 4:17 in the morning with the pump pulling at me and the dark pressing in. I focused on the ceiling, on counting the water stains, on the hum of the machine, anything to keep the memory from crawling up my throat.

I watched the milk drip slowly into the bottles. Steady. Mechanical, like tears that had learned to fall on schedule. When the bottles were full and I felt hollowed out, I removed the pump, sealed everything, and packed the bottles into the small cooler I kept by the bed. The milk wasn't for my baby. It was for someone else's child, a baby without a face or a name.

It was the only thing I had left to give, and most days, the giving was the only thing that made me feel like I still existed.

My phone alarm cut through the quiet and I silenced it fast, one slap of my palm against the screen. In the bathroom, the mirror ambushed me, the same as always. Pale skin. Bruised circles under my eyes so dark they looked painted on. My hair hung limp around a face I barely recognized, thick and dark and tangled from a restless night. My body didn't feel like mine anymore. It felt borrowed, like someone had rearranged me and walked away before checking the damage.

But life doesn't wait for you to feel ready. Life keeps moving whether you do or not.

I stepped into the shower. The water came out scalding. I'd cranked the handle all the way left on purpose. It hit my skin as punishment, and I stood there, letting it burn, because at least the pain on the outside matched a wound I could see. At least it numbed the other thing for a while. I stayed under it too long, the same as always, until my skin was pink and raw and the steam had fogged the mirror into a merciful blank.

Afterward, I dried my dark hair, tied it back, and wrapped a scarf around it to pull it into a bun that would hold through the day. I reached into the closet and pulled out the plum dress, the one that used to fall just right along my hips, that used to make me feel like I'd chosen correctly for once. It didn't fit that way anymore. The fabric pulled tight across my chest, hugged my stomach, clung to my hips like it was trying to remind me of every pound my body had gained and refused to let go of. I tugged at the hem. Adjusted the neckline. Turned sideways in the mirror and turned away again, faster.

I wore it anyway. I didn't have the money for a new wardrobe. Everything about this chapter of my life felt wrong,

4

like wearing a costume of the woman I used to be, hoping nobody would notice the seams splitting.

I grabbed the cooler and stepped out.

The parking lot was cold and gray, a light mist clinging to the asphalt. My old second-hand Honda Civic sat in its usual spot, faded blue, dent in the bumper, a car that seemed to apologize for itself just by existing. It was all I could afford now. Before the divorce, I'd had a different life. A different car. A different version of myself that I couldn't afford to think about while driving.

The milk bank was on my way to the shop. I parked, grabbed the cooler, and walked in. Inside, everything was spotless, white walls, labeled shelves, the hum of commercial refrigerators behind a glass partition. Clean in a way that made you believe the world still had order, even when yours didn't.

The director met me near the entrance. She was a small woman with reading glasses pushed up on her forehead and a smile that knew more than it let on, warm, but careful. The smile of someone who had learned not to push.

"Rose, good to see you." She kept her tone soft, careful, unsure how fragile I was today.

I forced a smile back, the same one I'd been handing out for weeks, cheap and automatic. "This week's milk." I held out the cooler.

Her hands brushed mine as she took it, her grip light but steady, like she understood that even small gestures mattered to someone running on fumes. "Thank you." She met my eyes. "Really."

I nodded. Lingered for a moment. For a moment, purpose warmed the hollow place in my chest. This milk would reach a baby somewhere. A real baby, alive and hungry and needing.

That quiet thought was enough to keep me standing upright. A reminder that, despite every broken thing behind me, I was still making a difference. Even if it was the smallest one in the world.

I turned and left before the feeling could dissolve. The door swung shut behind me, and the gray morning swallowed me again.

The flower shop sat on a corner lot three blocks east of downtown. Small awning, hand-painted sign, window display I refreshed every Monday whether I felt like it or not. I parked out front, unlocked the door, and pushed it open. The bell above it jingled. A bright, stubborn little sound that echoed through the empty space like it hadn't gotten the memo about my mood.

The air inside hit me first. Roses, gardenias, the green-water smell of fresh-cut stems sitting in their buckets overnight. The colors came next. Deep reds, soft pinks, whites so bright they almost hurt. They clashed with the heavy thing I carried inside me, all that brightness against all that gray, but I'd learned to let them exist side by side. I'd had this shop once before. Lost it. Clawed it back with nothing but stubbornness and a business loan that made my stomach hurt every time I thought about the interest. But it was mine again, and that was enough for now.

I flicked on the lights. The fluorescents buzzed to life over-head, that industrial hum that had become its own kind of comfort. I walked past the displays, my fingers brushing the petals as I moved. Soft. Cool. Velvety under my fingertips in a way that pulled me back into my body when everything else wanted to float away.

I grabbed my apron from the hook by the register. The

worn fabric felt familiar, stained at the pocket from years of handling green stems, fraying at the ties, soft as something that had been washed a hundred times. I tied it behind my back and forced myself into the rhythm. Snip. Arrange. Mist. Repeat.

Arranging bouquets came naturally by now. My hands knew what to do even when my head was somewhere else, trimming stems at an angle, adjusting vases so the tallest blooms sat in the back, spraying leaves until the mist collected on my skin in tiny cold pinpricks. The motions were automatic. The comfort was real, even if it was thin.

But no matter how busy I kept my hands, my thoughts still drifted. They always drifted. Back to the man who had stood in this shop once and smiled at me like I was the only person in the room. The man who had taken the last bit of happiness I'd had and crushed it between his fingers without even flinching.

I didn't let myself think his name. Not today.

Customers came and went through the morning, a slow trickle that picked up around eleven. Their faces blurred together, polite smiles, quick transactions, the rustle of tissue paper and the crinkle of cellophane. The shop was busier than most Tuesdays, but I couldn't feel any of it. Each sale felt like going through the motions. Smile when they hand you the cash, nod when they comment on the arrangement, say *thank you* and mean nothing by it. Inside, I was just surviving. Showing up because the alternative was staying in that apartment with the water-stained ceiling and the pump and the silence, and I wasn't ready to find out what would happen if I stopped moving.

Katie stepped through the door around noon. The bell jingled and she blew in with it, damp jacket, bag slung over one shoulder, bangs falling across her forehead in a way she'd been complaining about for weeks. Her eyes found me immediately, scanning, assessing, filing away whatever she saw before I could arrange my face into something convincing.

Today there was something extra in her look. She paused by the counter, her coat half-shrugged off, and her expression softened into something that made me want to look away.

"This dress." She motioned toward my plum outfit with one hand, the other still wrestling her sleeve. "Really brings out the brown in your eyes. And your hair, it's darker against this color." She tilted her head, a small smile tugging at the corner of her mouth. "You look good, Rose."

I tugged at the fabric stretched across my stomach, my fingers worrying the seam. "Thanks," I mumbled. The word felt stiff coming out. A compliment received and not understood, a gift I didn't know how to hold. But I appreciated it. I appreciated her.

Katie hung her jacket on the hook beside mine and turned back, her eyes gentle but direct. "You alright?" She folded her arms lightly across her chest, leaning one hip against the counter, not crowding me, just present.

I gave her the smile. The one I'd been giving everyone. "Just tired. One of those days, you know?"

Her lips pressed together, and I could see the next question forming behind her teeth. The real one, the one she wanted to ask. But she swallowed it. She nodded once, slow. "I'm here if you need to talk." Her gaze held mine for a beat longer than casual, then she let it go, pushing off the counter and moving toward the back to clock in.

I exhaled through my nose. Grateful. Grateful she didn't push. I didn't have the energy for a heart-to-heart. Not today, not when I was balanced on the edge of something I couldn't name, and the wrong question might send me over.

The afternoon crawled. A steady stream of faces, some browsing, some picking up orders, some rushing in with the panicked energy of people who'd forgotten an anniversary or a birthday and needed beauty in the next five minutes. Katie stayed busy at the other end of the shop, flipping through sample books with a woman planning her wedding flowers. I could hear their voices. Katie's warm and encouraging, the bride's bright with an excitement that belonged to a different lifetime. But they sounded far away, muffled, like I was hearing them through a wall.

I kept my head down. Kept my hands moving. Because if I stopped — if I let myself think — the tightness in my chest would come back, and this time it might not leave.

The bell chimed. An older man shuffled in, moving slowly, his hands tucked into the pockets of a corduroy jacket that had seen better decades. He stopped just inside the door and looked around the shop like he'd walked into a cathedral, over-whelmed, reverent, completely lost.

"I need help." He pulled one hand free to gesture vaguely at everything. His voice was soft, a little rough at the edges. "It's my wife's birthday. Fifty-two years. I never know what to get."

I came around the counter and walked him through the roses. Past the standard reds that every man defaults to, to the deep burgundy ones in the back, the ones with petals so dark they looked like velvet in the right light. I picked three stems, trimmed them, added a few sprigs of baby's breath, and wrapped them in brown paper tied with twine.

His fingers trembled slightly when he took the bouquet. He

held it up and studied the blooms, and his whole expression changed. The lines around his eyes deepened, his mouth softened, and for a second I could see him imagining the woman who'd been beside him for fifty-two years, the look she'd give him when he walked through the door with flowers. "She's going to love these," he murmured, almost to himself.

I nodded, my throat tight. "She will."

He left. The bell chimed behind him.

A few minutes later, a boy came in. Sixteen, maybe seventeen, cheeks flushed red, the collar of his jacket turned up like he was trying to disappear inside it. He asked for daisies. His voice cracked on the word.

I pulled a bunch from the bucket, shook the water off the stems, and tied a white ribbon around them while he stood there picking at his thumbnail, his eyes darting toward the door every few seconds like he was timing something, or someone.

I held out the bouquet. He took it and grinned, wide and sudden, a grin that only shows up when you're sixteen and terrified and about to do something brave. He was out the door before I could say *good luck,* nearly tripping over the welcome mat on his way.

On a different day — a better day — I would have held those moments close. I would have let them remind me why I loved this work, why flowers mattered, why the giving and receiving of something beautiful between two people was worth building a life around. I used to feel it. Used to carry those small bright things home with me like coins in my pocket.

But today I was somewhere beneath the surface, moving through the hours as though through water, slowly, heavily, everything muted and distant. No matter how many bouquets I arranged or how many times I breathed in the sweetness of fresh-cut stems, the ache wouldn't lift. It sat low in my chest, stubborn and patient, refusing to budge. Refusing to let me move on.

I closed the register at the end of the day and stood there in the quiet shop, surrounded by flowers that were bright and alive and completely indifferent to the fact that I was neither.

Chapter Two

My hands throbbed from the day's work, knuckles stiff, a blister forming on my right thumb from the shears. The whole day had passed without me, customers had come and gone, stems had been trimmed, orders had gone out, and my hands had done the work while the rest of me circled the same drain. By the time Katie waved goodnight through the glass door, my body was tired in the ordinary way. But my mind was worse. My mind was a room I didn't want to be in.

I looked around the quiet shop. The roses and lilies were still bright — absurdly bright, offensively alive — their colors clashing with the gray thing that had settled behind my eyes. The scent of them lingered, that thick sweetness mixing with the green smell of water sitting too long in ceramic vases, and I couldn't connect with any of it. I stood in a painting and felt nothing for the colors.

I sank into the worn leather chair behind the counter. The cushion exhaled beneath me, old and tired, and I pressed my thumbs into my temples until it hurt. The tension wasn't just in my head. It sat in my jaw, my shoulders, the tight cords of my neck, wound through my body, wire pulled too tight.

It wasn't just him.

That was the thing nobody understood, the thing I hadn't said out loud to anyone yet. The grief over the man I'd married. That was a wound I could name, could press on and know the edges of. But there was another wound underneath it, deeper, uglier, and it belonged to someone else entirely.

Her.

The bitterness rose in my throat like something physical, something I could taste, sour as old pennies, the taste of something already dead. She'd come into my life with that smile. The one she used when she wanted to look harmless. And behind it, she'd been taking everything apart, beam by beam, until the whole structure collapsed and I was standing in the rubble wondering how I hadn't heard the cracking.

She didn't stumble into the affair. She walked into it with her eyes open. She chose it. She chose him. She chose to sit across from me and laugh and lie and pretend nothing was different while the life I'd built was burning down behind her.

My anger wasn't just for Phoenix. It was for her. The one who had destroyed everything I trusted with nothing more than a smile and zero guilt.

I stood up too fast and the blood rushed to my head, darkening the edges of my vision for a second. I grabbed my coat from the hook by the door. My coat settled across my shoulders, heavy wool smelling faintly of old perfume.

Outside, the cool autumn air hit my face and I pulled the coat tighter, feeling the chill settle into my bones. The streets were slick from rain that had fallen while I was inside, the pavement shining wet under the streetlights. Reflections of the lampposts stretched and warped in the puddles, long, distorted shapes that moved when the wind rippled the water. My car sat a few blocks away, parked where the meter was cheaper, a small daily humiliation I'd learned to stop noticing.

Tonight was therapy. Dr. Mitchell had been a lifeline for months. The one hour a week where I didn't have to perform *fine* for anyone. But no amount of her careful questions could dissolve the thing simmering inside me. This anger didn't dissolve. It hardened.

My phone buzzed in my coat pocket. I didn't look. I didn't want anyone else's voice in my head right now, not even as text on a screen. I needed the quiet. Needed to sit with the ugly feeling before I walked into that office and tried to shape it into words.

The drive was short and silent. The engine hummed beneath me, the sound steady and low, blending with the thoughts that kept circling, the same loop, the same images, the same sick feeling in my gut that never quite went away. The streets were nearly empty, just a few headlights passing in the opposite direction, their glow smearing across the wet windshield. I knew these roads well. Every turn, every stoplight. They led me to the one place I'd come to trust.

Dr. Mitchell's office sat on a quiet block at the edge of downtown, tucked between a law firm and a shuttered bookstore. The building was small, two stories, large windows, a converted house that still carried its domestic bones beneath the professional signage. During the day, natural light poured through those windows and made the waiting room feel like somewhere you might actually want to sit. Tonight, the windows glowed soft and amber, and the warmth behind them promised something.

I parked and killed the engine. Sat there for a moment with my hands on the wheel, staring at the lit windows, preparing myself for something that was going to hurt in a useful way. Then I grabbed my bag and went inside.

The waiting room was simple. Two upholstered chairs, a side table with a box of tissues and a stack of magazines nobody read, and a framed print of a seascape that was supposed to be calming but mostly just reminded me that I hadn't been to the ocean in years. I approached the reception desk and the woman behind it — mid-fifties, short gray hair, reading glasses on a chain — smiled with the practiced warmth of someone who greeted anxious people for a living.

"Good evening, Rose." She tapped something on her screen without looking at it. "Dr. Mitchell will see you shortly."

I nodded and sat. The fabric of the chair was cool against the backs of my arms, and I pressed my palms flat against my thighs, trying to keep my fingers from fidgeting. The minutes stretched, and with each one, the knot in my chest pulled tighter. It wasn't dread, exactly. More like the feeling before a confession. The knowledge that you're about to say something you can't take back.

The inner door opened and Dr. Mitchell appeared. She was tall, early sixties, with silver hair cropped close and a face that never flinched. No matter what you put in front of it. Her eyes were steady and brown and they found mine immediately, offering the same quiet welcome she always did. No fuss, no performance, just the assurance that whatever I brought through that door, she could hold it.

She led me down a short hallway to her office. The room was small, lined with bookshelves so full they bowed in the middle, and furnished with two chairs, a desk she never sat behind, and a window that faced the street. At night, the view was just headlights and streetlamps, their reflections floating in the dark glass like distant signals. She motioned to the chair across from hers. The one I always took, the one with the dent in the cushion that was probably mine by now.

"Good evening, Rose." She settled into her seat, crossed one ankle over the other, and rested a leather notebook on her knee. Her pen was uncapped but still. "How are you feeling today?"

I didn't answer right away. I took a breath that was supposed to be steadying and came out ragged instead. My fingers found the hem of my sleeve and started working it, rolling the fabric between my thumb and forefinger. A habit I didn't remember picking up.

"Tired." The word came out flat. I tried again, searching for the one that actually fit. "And... angry."

Dr. Mitchell nodded once, slow, holding the silence long enough for the words to land. "I understand. You've been carrying a great deal." She tilted her head slightly, her pen still motionless on the notebook. "Do you want to talk about what's feeding the anger tonight?"

I looked down at my hands. The skin around my thumbnail was raw where I'd been picking at it without realizing. "It's not just Phoenix." I pressed my thumbnail into the raw skin around it.

His name dropped into the room and the silence rippled out from it. Phoenix. My husband. My *ex*-husband. The man I'd built a life around, only to discover the foundation was rotten and the whole thing was always going to come down.

"It's not just him," I repeated, quieter this time, the tightness at the back of my throat threatening to close off the words. "It's her. The one who came between us."

Dr. Mitchell leaned forward, not much, just enough to close an inch of the distance between us, her elbows settling on her knees. "It sounds like the betrayal runs deeper because it wasn't just him."

"Exactly." I pressed the word out through clenched teeth. "She knew what she was doing, Dr. Mitchell. Every second of it. She didn't stumble into it. She didn't get swept up in something. She *calculated.* She looked me in the eye and smiled at me while she was tearing my life apart."

My fingers had abandoned the sleeve and were now gripping the arm of the chair, knuckles blanching. I forced myself to loosen my hold, to breathe, to not spiral. But the anger had its own momentum tonight, and I was barely keeping ahead of it.

"Tell me about Phoenix." Her tone softened after a moment, gentler now, more careful, because she knew it was fragile. "About how things changed."

I closed my eyes. The memories didn't come in order. They never did. They came in flashes, sense memories, fragments of feeling, snapshots with the context ripped away.

"He used to love me." I hated how small the words sounded. "In the beginning, he loved me like I was the only person in the world. He took me everywhere, dinners, events, meetings. He wanted me beside him. He was proud of me." I paused. My teeth had been pressed together so long the ache had set in, and each word had to push past it. "I never really understood why he chose me. I'm not. I wasn't someone who turned heads. But he chose me, and I let myself believe that was enough."

Dr. Mitchell's pen moved for the first time, a small note, quick and private. She didn't look down at the page. "And when did things begin to shift?"

"When I got pregnant." The words came out flat, stripped of everything except the fact. "I was thirty-seven. High risk. But I was happy." I swallowed. "He wasn't."

The room felt smaller suddenly, the bookshelves pressing closer. I stared at the window, at my own faint reflection hovering in the dark glass, a woman in a plum dress that didn't fit right, sitting in a therapist's chair, trying to explain how she'd been unmade.

"At first it was subtle. He'd cancel plans. Make excuses not to be around. And then it stopped being subtle." My voice dropped, not because I wanted it to. Because the memory had weight, and it dragged my voice down with it. "He stopped taking me anywhere. Especially once I started showing. He'd leave for work, for events, for dinners, and I'd be at home. Alone. Every time I asked why, he'd brush it off, *You'd be uncomfortable. It's not your scene right now.*" I mimicked his tone without meaning to, that dismissive smoothness he'd perfected, and the sound of it coming from my own mouth made my stomach turn. "Like being pregnant made me invisible, like growing his child made me something he needed to hide."

My reflection in the window stared back at me, and I looked away from it. The sight of myself — this version of myself, worn down, sitting in this chair — was harder to face than the memories.

"He made me feel like I'd done something wrong by changing," I whispered. "By getting bigger. By being pregnant, like my body had betrayed him somehow." I tugged at the

18

fabric of my dress, the plum cotton straining across my chest. "I tried so hard to keep up. To still be the woman he wanted. But nothing I did was ever enough. I could feel him pulling away, and the harder I reached for him, the faster he went."

Dr. Mitchell set her pen down on the notebook, a deliberate motion. Her hands folded in her lap, open and still. "That kind of withdrawal during a pregnancy, it's a profound abandonment, Rose. You deserved support. You deserved presence."

The word *deserved* sat between us, a truth I didn't know how to hold. I'd spent so long believing I'd earned what happened. That if I'd been prettier, thinner, less needy, more interesting, he would have stayed. That the failure was mine.

"And the pregnancy..." Dr. Mitchell uncrossed her ankles and leaned forward slightly, her fingers lacing together over the notebook. Her tone was careful now, measured, the tone she used when she approached the places I'd sealed off. "We've touched on this before, but—"

"I don't talk about that night." The words came out fast, clipped, hard, a door slamming shut. My hands had gone tight in my lap again, fingers lacing together so hard the knuckles ached. I could feel it right there, pressing against the wall I'd built. The hospital lights, the sound of machines, the moment they told me. The moment everything ended.

I shook my head once, sharp. "Not tonight."

Dr. Mitchell nodded without hesitation, respecting the boundary completely, without making me feel like I'd failed by setting it. "Of course."

The silence resettled. I breathed into it, willing my pulse to slow, willing the fragments to sink back down where I kept them.

"Let's come back to the anger." Dr. Mitchell let a moment

pass, her tone resettling into its steady rhythm. "The woman you mentioned. You said she came into your life and took what she wanted. When you think about confronting her, what does that look like for you?"

I exhaled. The question should have been simple, but it cracked something open. "I don't know. I want to confront her, but I don't know if it'll help. She's already done the damage." My shoulders dropped, the anger giving way — just slightly — to exhaustion, plain and bare. "I doubt she even cares. She moves through people. Uses them and leaves. And the worst part is. I *let* her in. I trusted her. That's what makes it unbearable. What she did was one thing. That I never saw it coming was worse."

Dr. Mitchell picked up her pen again, turning it slowly between her fingers. "Confronting her doesn't have to be about getting an apology. You may never get one." She let that sit. "It's about finding peace for yourself, Rose. Letting go of the hold she has on you. Right now, she's living rent-free in your head, and that's not sustainable. Confrontation — when you're ready, on your terms — can be about reclaiming the space she's occupying."

I stared at the dark window, at the blurred city lights beyond it, floating and indistinct. "I just don't want to carry this forever." My voice came out softer than I expected, the anger thinning into honesty, or maybe fear. "I don't want her living in my head for the rest of my life."

Dr. Mitchell's expression warmed, the lines around her eyes deepening. "That's important, Rose. Recognizing that you want to move forward, that's not a small thing. It won't happen all at once. But the fact that you're sitting here, saying these words, means you're already on the path."

I nodded slowly. The words sank into me. Not an answer. A door left slightly ajar. I didn't know if I believed her. I didn't know if confrontation would give me anything other than another wound. But for the first time in months, the anger was no longer a cage. It was a compass, pointing somewhere. Toward *her*.

The air outside the office was colder than when I'd arrived. The wind had picked up while I was inside, scattering dead leaves across the parking lot in brittle, scraping spirals. I pulled my coat tighter and walked toward the car, my footsteps quick on the wet asphalt.

The anger stayed. Now it had a direction. It was no longer the formless thing that had been eating me alive for months. It had edges now. A needle lodged in my chest, pointing north.

I knew what I needed to do. I didn't know when. I didn't know how. But the woman who had torn my life open — who had sat across from me, smiling, lying, taking — was going to hear what I had to say. I didn't need her to hear it. I didn't need the apology that would never come.

I needed it for me.

My steps quickened across the parking lot, my heels clicking sharp and fast against the pavement. The wind caught my scarf and pulled it sideways, and I didn't bother fixing it. I got in the car, shut the door, and sat in the silence for a moment, just me and the ticking of the cooling engine and the dark beyond the windshield.

Then I turned the key and drove home.

Chapter Three

Back at the apartment, I dropped my bag by the door, kicked off my shoes, and stood there for a moment in the dark entryway, listening to nothing but silence.

I moved through the rooms on muscle memory. Hung my coat. Lit the pumpkin spice candles on the kitchen counter, three of them, the cheap ones from the dollar store that smelled more like cinnamon than pumpkin, but I'd been burning them since October started and the ritual was all that mattered now. The match hissed, the flames caught, and the warm glow spread across the countertop without warming anything inside me.

I made dinner because the clock said I should. Pasta, butter, salt, a meal that required nothing and gave back less. I ate standing at the counter, fork scraping against the bowl, chewing without registering taste. Three bites in, I stopped pretending and scraped the rest into the trash.

Later, I sat in the dark on the edge of my bed, the soft hum of the breast pump filling the room. Rain had started, a quiet, steady tapping against the window, the drops catching light from the streetlamp outside and sliding down the glass in crooked silver lines. The pump's rhythm and the rain, those two sounds held me in place, kept me from sinking too far into the silence. Without them, I wasn't sure what I'd hear. My own thoughts, probably. And those were worse than any quiet.

The ache in my chest was familiar by now, the pressure, the fullness, the body remembering something the mind was trying to forget. I stared at the wall and let the machine work, my hands loose in my lap, my breathing shallow. This was the loneliest hour. Not the waking at 4 a.m., not the empty shop after closing. This. Sitting in the dark, hooked up to a machine designed for a purpose I no longer had, producing something meant for a child who would never drink it.

Then my phone buzzed on the nightstand. The screen lit the room in a cold blue flash, and the name on it stopped my blood.

Maya.

My fingers curled into fists against my thighs. Maya. The name sat in my chest like a coal. Maya, who was supposed to be my best friend. Maya, who I'd known since college, who'd stood beside me at my wedding, who'd held my hand when I told her I was pregnant and squealed like the news was hers to celebrate. Maya, who had looked me in the eye a hundred times since then and never once flinched.

Maya, the one who had betrayed me.

She didn't know I'd found out. During the divorce, I'd been too consumed with grief to deal with her, too shattered by the baby, by the hospital, by the papers that arrived like a final insult. There had been no room left for anger. Only pain, filling every corner of me until there was nothing else. But the anger had been there all along, underneath, waiting. Growing in the dark the way mold grows. Silently, steadily, feeding on every-thing I tried to bury.

I stared at the phone. My fingers hovered over the screen, trembling. I didn't want to read it. I didn't want her words back in my life, didn't want her casual tone polluting the fragile quiet I'd built around myself. But I couldn't stop my thumb from moving.

I opened the message.

Hey Rose! I know things have been weird between us, and I thought maybe this could help us reset. We're planning a Halloween getaway at this amazing plantation estate, a couple of nights over the holiday. It's a huge old mansion with full-on ghost-tour vibes. You deserve something fun after everything. Let me do this for you, it's gonna be great. Let me know.

My stomach turned over, slow and sour. The cheerfulness of it. The exclamation marks, the breezy tone, the *we'd love for you to join us*, as though she were inviting me to brunch. How could she type those words? How could she sit wherever she was sitting and compose that message as though every-thing between us was fine, as though she hadn't gutted my life and left the mess for me to clean up alone?

Another message followed, the notification sliding down the screen before I could close the first one.

I've added you to our WhatsApp group so you can see the details. Hope to see you there!

WhatsApp.

The word hit something inside me. A tripwire I didn't know was still live. WhatsApp. The app. The messages. The photos.

And just like that, the memory I'd been holding at arm's length for months broke through the wall and flooded in.

24

It was a Tuesday. I remembered that because Tuesdays were the day Phoenix worked from home, and I'd been trying to time my naps around his schedule so he wouldn't hear me crying. I was eight months along by then, heavy and slow, my ankles swollen, my back aching from carrying the weight of a baby that felt like it was sitting directly on my spine. I'd come downstairs for water and found his phone on the kitchen counter.

Just sitting there. Screen down, like it was nothing.

Maybe he wanted me to find it. Maybe he'd gotten careless. Or maybe — and this was the thought that twisted deepest — he simply didn't care anymore whether I knew or not.

A knot coiled in my stomach, a cold certainty, whispering to leave it alone. My fingers trembled as I reached for the phone. Every nerve in my body screamed to put it down, walk away, go back upstairs and pretend I hadn't seen it. But I couldn't. The suspicion had been eating at me for weeks. The late nights, his phone always on silent, the way he'd avoid my eyes when I asked where he'd been. I'd told myself it was hormones. Paranoia. The kind of irrational fear that pregnancy breeds.

But my gut knew. My gut had known for months.

I unlocked the phone. Scrolled past the business emails, past the calendar reminders, past the surface of his life that he kept polished and presentable. And then I found the messages. The WhatsApp thread.

The photos loaded first.

Her. Sitting in his car, legs crossed, hair perfect, laughing at something he'd said, or something she'd said to make him laugh. The ease in her posture. The familiarity. They were at a restaurant I'd never heard of, a place with low lighting and white tablecloths. Somewhere he used to take me, before my belly grew too big for him to stomach.

I kept scrolling. My thumb moved on its own, dragging the screen upward, each new image a fist to the sternum. Close-ups first, body parts, skin, curves. Sent to him like invitations, like promises. Then full photos of her smiling, dressed in outfits I recognized. Fitted, elegant, the silhouettes I used to wear before my body stopped cooperating with his standards. She looked happy. She looked like she'd won something.

And there he was in the background of some of the photos, giving her the moments that used to be mine. The dinners. The smiles. The attention. Everything I'd been starving for, served up to someone else while I sat at home in sweatpants, rubbing my belly, waiting for him to come back.

My hands shook so hard the phone nearly slipped from my grip. I kept scrolling. More photos. More of her. She smiled in every single one, the same confident, unbothered smile. The smile of a woman who had everything she wanted and wasn't sorry about how she'd gotten it.

Then I saw the dates.

The timestamps on the messages. The metadata on the photos. And the floor tilted beneath me.

They weren't old. They weren't from before me, before us, before the ring and the vows and the nursery painted seafoam green. They were *recent*. Weeks recent. Taken while I was pregnant. While I was carrying his child, growing his family inside my body, he had been with her. Laughing, eating, touching, living a parallel life I knew nothing about.

I tried to tell myself there was an explanation. A misunderstanding. A detail I was reading wrong. But the dates were right there, glowing on the screen, and they matched the nights he'd come home late smelling like cologne he hadn't been wearing when he left.

"Phoenix!" The scream tore out of me before I could shape it into words. Cracked, the sound of bone giving way.

He didn't rush in. He didn't come running. He walked, slow, unhurried, a man approaching a mild inconvenience. He appeared in the kitchen doorway with papers in one hand, his reading glasses pushed up on his forehead, his expression the carefully neutral mask of someone who had already decided this conversation wasn't worth his full attention.

"What is it?" He didn't look up from the papers. His thumb kept its place on the page, holding his spot.

I held up the phone. The screen was still lit, the photos still glowing, her face, her body, their restaurant, their life. "What the hell is this?" My arm shook with the effort of holding it steady.

Phoenix sighed through his nose, a short, irritated exhale, dismissive, the sound reserved for a child who has interrupted something important. He glanced at the phone, then at me, and one eyebrow lifted, not in alarm, not in guilt. In mild amusement.

"Put the phone down, Rose." His tone was flat. A command dressed as advice.

"Put the phone *down?*" The words came out trembling, each one fighting through the pressure building in my throat. "You don't even care, do you? You don't even—"

He shrugged. One shoulder. Barely a movement at all. Then a small sound escaped him, close to a laugh, close enough to curdle my blood. A chuckle. He *chuckled.*

"You were going to find out sooner or later."

The room tilted. I blinked, trying to catch up, trying to

make the words fit into some version of reality where my husband hadn't just confirmed everything with the casual disinterest of a man canceling a dinner reservation. No denial. No apology. No scramble for an excuse. Just the truth, dropped at my feet like something he'd been carrying too long and was glad to be rid of.

"You've been cheating on me." I barely recognized my own voice, cracked down the middle, splitting at the seams. "While I'm pregnant. With your baby."

Phoenix's expression shifted. The amusement drained away, replaced by contempt. His eyes narrowed, and his mouth thinned in that way it did when he was about to say something he knew would leave a mark. He took a step toward me, closing the distance, using his height the same as always, wanting me to feel small.

"Don't you dare raise your voice at me, Rose." The words came out low and sharp, a blade wrapped in silk. Then his lip curled — a sneer, ugly and deliberate — and he looked me up and down. Slowly. From my swollen feet to my round belly to my face, flushed and wet with tears I hadn't felt start.

"What did you expect?" He let the question hang for a second, savoring it. "Look at yourself." Another pause. His gaze dropped to my stomach and stayed there. "You're a whale. This is pathetic."

The words didn't hit like a slap, sudden, sharp, over. They hit the way cold water does, everywhere at once, soaking through every layer until there was nowhere left that was dry. *Pathetic.* That's what he thought of me. That's what I was to him. I wasn't his wife to him anymore. I wasn't the mother of his child. A whale. A bloated, ridiculous thing that had the nerve to expect love.

"I'm pathetic?" My voice cracked, but I didn't care anymore, didn't care about the tears, the snot, the way my chin was trembling. "I'm carrying your child, Phoenix."

He stepped closer. Close enough that I could smell his cologne, the expensive one, the one he'd been wearing to see her. "I expected you to keep it together." Each word was measured and cold, set down one at a time. "Women get pregnant all the time. Most of them take care of themselves." His eyes swept over me again, and his mouth twisted. "But you... you just let yourself go."

I'd tried. God, I had tried. I'd tried to eat right, to exercise when my body would let me, to keep my hair done and my face presentable, to still be the woman on his arm even when standing up made my back scream. I had tried every single day to shrink myself back into the shape he wanted, and every single day my body had told me no, this is what carrying a life looks like, this is what it costs, and he had looked at that cost and found it disgusting.

I stared at him through blurred vision, tears running hot down my cheeks. "You disgust me."

Phoenix shrugged. The same one-shoulder shrug. Not a flinch, not a flicker, not the smallest crack in that polished, contemptuous surface. "If you're gonna get emotional, we're done here." He turned halfway, already moving on, already filing this away as a scene he'd rather not revisit.

That's when the pain hit.

Sharp. Sudden. A blade of fire sliding through my lower abdomen, so bright and immediate that the world whited out for a second. The phone slipped from my fingers and thudded onto the carpet. I gasped — a wet, choking sound — and my hands flew to my stomach. My knees buckled. The floor came up fast, cold tile slamming against my kneecaps, and the impact sent a shockwave through my body that made everything inside me clench.

I felt the blood before I saw it. Warm. Wet. Spreading through the fabric of my sweatpants, pooling beneath me on the kitchen floor, thick and dark, the color of something that should have stayed inside.

"Phoenix..." I reached for him. My hand was shaking so badly it looked like someone else's. My voice was barely there, thin, reedy, a sound scraped from the bottom of an empty well. "Something's wrong. Something's—"

He didn't move. He stood there, three feet away, and looked down at me on the floor — at the blood, at my outstretched hand, at the terror on my face — and his expression didn't change, not one degree. It was the look of a man watching something inconvenient happen to someone else.

"I'll call an ambulance." Flat. Functional. He picked up his phone — the same phone, the one with her photos still on it — and dialed like he was ordering takeout.

That was the last thing I heard before the dark swallowed me whole.

When I opened my eyes, I was in a hospital bed. The lights were too bright, the sheets too stiff, and the room smelled like antiseptic and institutional soap. I didn't know how long I'd been there. Hours. Maybe longer. The clock on the wall said it was past midnight.

Phoenix was gone. The nurses told me he'd filled out the admission forms, spoken briefly with the attending physician, and left. No forwarding message. No indication of when he'd return.

He didn't return.

It was a nurse — young, kind-eyed, with braids pinned up under her cap — who told me. She sat on the edge of my bed and took my hand, and the answer was already in her face before she opened her mouth. Her thumb pressed into my knuckle. Her lips pressed together. The room narrowed to just her face and the terrible softness in it.

The baby was gone.

I don't remember making a sound, but I must have, because two more nurses came in. I cried until my ribs ached. Until my throat was raw and my eyes swelled shut and there was nothing left, no tears, no sound, just a hollow, ringing emptiness that settled into my bones and stayed. The nurses held me. Strangers held me. They rubbed my back and said things I couldn't hear, and they were the only ones there.

I stayed two days. On the second morning, a different nurse came in carrying a sealed envelope. She held it out with an apologetic expression, the kind people wear when they know they're handing you something that will hurt.

Divorce papers. Phoenix had sent them over, no visit, no phone call, no note. Just the papers, delivered to my hospital bed while I was still bleeding from the loss of his child. He'd signed them already. Clean, decisive strokes in black ink, like he'd been waiting for the right moment.

He was done. He had walked away from everything — from me, from the baby, from the marriage — with the same ease he'd walked into that kitchen when I confronted him. As if none of it had ever been real. As if the life we'd built had been a draft he'd decided not to publish.

And Maya.

Maya was the woman in those photos.

The realization hadn't come all at once. It came in pieces,

during the divorce proceedings, during the long, sleepless nights that followed, during the slow and agonizing process of combing through the wreckage and trying to understand how everything had fallen apart so completely.

The woman laughing in Phoenix's car. The one at the restaurant I'd never been to. The close-ups, the outfits, the confident smile that said *I have what I want and I'm not sorry.* It was Maya. My best friend. The woman who'd held my hand at the gender reveal, who'd helped me pick out the crib, who'd texted me *thinking of you* on the nights Phoenix was supposedly working late. The nights he was with her.

She'd sat across from me at brunches and baby showers and long, rambling phone calls and never once — not a single time — showed a crack in the facade. She'd listened to me worry about Phoenix pulling away and told me it was just stress, that men get weird during pregnancies, that everything would be fine once the baby came. She'd been the voice in my ear saying *trust him, trust this, trust me,* and every word had been a lie layered on top of a lie, stacked so high I couldn't see over the top.

She'd destroyed my marriage. She'd helped destroy my family. And she'd done it all with that smile — warm enough to make betrayal look impossible — the smile I'd trusted since we were twenty-two and swapping notes in the back of a lecture hall.

Phoenix had shattered my heart. But Maya. Maya had poisoned the ground it grew from.

I stared at her text on the screen, my teeth pressed together so hard my molars ached. The breast pump hummed beside me, forgotten. The rain tapped its steady rhythm against the window. And inside me, something that had been locked away

— a fury dark and patient and coiled very, very tight — began to unfurl.

She didn't know I knew. That was the thing. Through the entire divorce, through all the grief and the hospital and the papers and the rebuilding, I had never confronted her. I hadn't had the strength. The loss of the baby had consumed everything, left no room for anything except the business of not dying from sadness. Maya had texted me during that time, casual check-ins, sympathetic messages, the occasional *I'm here for you* that made me want to throw my phone against the wall. But I'd never responded with the truth. I'd let her believe I was simply heartbroken over Phoenix, too shattered to see clearly.

She probably thought I was still broken. Still weak. Still the woman who couldn't stand on her own without someone else holding her up.

She had no idea what was waiting for her.

For the first time in months, grief was not the loudest thing in me. Sadness had kept me quiet. This wanted blood. Control came next, cold, clear-headed certainty. The rage I'd been burying beneath everything else was rising now, pushing up through the grief like a root through concrete, and it didn't feel destructive anymore. It felt like fuel.

I wanted her to see my face when I told her I knew. I wanted to watch the smile crack. I wanted to stand in front of her, steady and whole, and let her understand that the woman she'd betrayed hadn't disappeared, she'd been sharpening.

My thumb moved before my mind finished deciding. The letters appeared on the screen, one by one, each keystroke deliberate.

Sounds interesting. I'll join.

33

I tossed the phone onto the mattress. It bounced once and settled face-down, the screen going dark. My pulse was loud in my ears, fast, hard, the rhythm of a part of me waking up after a long, forced sleep. Adrenaline and fear braided together in my chest, pulling tight.

This was it. I was going to face her.

And this time, she wasn't going to see it coming.

Chapter Four

I'd been driving for nearly twelve hours. Oklahoma City to New Orleans, the longest stretch of road I'd ever sat behind a wheel for, and by hour nine my lower back had fused into a single knot of dull, grinding pain. My eyes burned from staring at the highway, and the white dashes on the asphalt had started to blur into one long, unbroken line.

I'd have lost my mind if I hadn't asked Katie to come.

The invitation had been last-minute. I'd called her the night before, half-expecting her to say no. But Katie had a way of hearing what you weren't saying, and whatever she heard in my voice that night was enough. She showed up at 6 a.m. with a thermos of coffee, a bag of gas station snacks, and zero questions about why we were driving twelve hours to spend Halloween at a plantation with people she'd never met.

She'd been excited at first. Buzzing, even, talking about plantation history, about whether the grounds would have those old live oaks draped in Spanish moss, about the ghost tours she'd seen advertised in the French Quarter. Her energy filled the car, and I let it, grateful for something to drown out the noise in my own head. But the further south we drove, the quieter she got. The interstate thinned to a two-lane highway. The strip malls and gas stations fell away. The landscape changed, farmland stretched flat on both sides first, then thicker growth, trees pressing closer to the road, their canopies stitching together overhead until the sky was just a narrow gray ribbon between the branches.

By the time we turned off the main road, Katie hadn't spoken in twenty minutes.

The road twisted through old farmland, cracked and pitted, a road that hadn't been repaved in a decade and didn't expect to be. The trees had closed in on both sides now, massive, gnarled things with trunks wider than the car, their branches reaching out over the road like arms trying to pull us in. Spanish moss hung from them, gray and still, swaying in a breeze I couldn't feel inside the car. The light dimmed even though it was still afternoon. Filtered through so much foliage that it turned the air a sickly green-gold, the light at the bottom of a pond.

When the mansion finally appeared at the end of the drive, Katie's face fell.

A wrought-iron sign arched over the entrance: Welcome to Willowcrest! The letters were rusted, and the exclamation mark hung crooked, too cheerful for rot. Beyond it, the mansion sat at the end of a long gravel drive. The stone walls had split in places. Ivy plugged the cracks. The roof sagged in the middle, and exposed beams showed through the missing tiles, black with damp. Wild fields stretched out on every side, tall grass, brambles, and the dead ribs of a garden that no one had loved in years.

Crows lined the iron fence. Dozens of them. One picked at

a torn strip of white paper caught on a spike, and for one sick second I thought of the nursing pads in my bag. As the car slowed on the gravel, none of the birds startled. Their heads turned with us, one by one, as if the house was taking attendance.

Katie's hand found the door handle and gripped it until her knuckles blanched white. She blew her bangs out of her face and turned to me.

"What the hell was she thinking?" Her eyes darted between the house and me, searching for an explanation I didn't have. "Is this some kind of joke?"

I had nothing. I shrugged.

She gave me a pointed look. The one she saved for moments when my decisions had personally inconvenienced her. "Girl, you dragged me out here." She jabbed a finger toward the mansion. "I need a raise and fewer work hours. Seriously."

I groaned and pinched the bridge of my nose, pressing until I saw spots. "I didn't think it would be this bad."

"You didn't *think?*" She shook her head, her bangs swinging. "This place looks like the set of a horror movie. Maya better have some damn good booze inside."

The front door creaked open before I could respond. And there was Maya. Standing in the doorway, grinning, arms spread wide as though this crumbling ruin behind her were a five-star resort and she was the concierge.

"Welcome to paradise!" she called out. Her laugh carried across the gravel, too cheerful for the dead air. It bounced off the house and came back sounding wrong. A recording of happiness played at the wrong speed.

My stomach clenched at the sight of her. She looked good.

She always looked good, that was part of her talent, part of what made her so dangerous. Hair blown out, makeup precise, wearing a cream-colored blouse that probably cost more than my car payment. The smile was wide and practiced and didn't reach her eyes. I knew that smile. I'd trusted that smile for years. And behind it, she'd been taking everything.

I kept my face neutral. Smiled back. The mask I'd been rehearsing in the rearview mirror for twelve hours.

Katie shot me a sideways look, her lips barely moving. "A raise. And fewer hours."

I sighed through my teeth. "I'll think about it."

We grabbed our bags from the trunk and followed Maya through the front door into the foyer. Just inside the entrance, a chipped porcelain bowl sat on a narrow table beneath the portraits, and I dropped my keys into it without thinking, too tired from the drive to keep them in my hand. The air inside hit us first, stale, heavy, carrying the smell of damp wood and decades of dust. It coated the back of my throat like a film. A chandelier hung from the ceiling, its crystals clouded and gray. It flickered weakly, barely denting the gloom. The bulbs buzzed, an unsteady, insect-like sound that set my teeth on edge.

The walls were lined with portraits. Oil paintings in heavy gilt frames, their colors darkened by age to near-uniformity. Every face a murky arrangement of pale skin and dark fabric, with eyes that seemed to track us as we moved through the space. You tell yourself it's an optical illusion, a trick of the brushwork, even as your body tightens and your pace quickens past them.

Katie glanced around and wrinkled her nose. "So, why this place?" She ran a finger along the edge of a side table, examined the gray dust on her fingertip, and wiped it on her jeans. "Did you get it for free or something?"

I caught her eye and nudged her elbow with mine, a small, quick warning. Maya was a bitch, but she was the one who'd invited us. I had to play nice. I was waiting for the right moment to say what I'd come to say, and that moment wasn't going to be the first five minutes. The confrontation had to land on my terms, not Maya's. So I kept the mask on and kept walking.

Maya gave a laugh that sounded like it had been rehearsed in front of a mirror. "It's Halloween, babe. This estate is supposed to be haunted." She waved one hand dismissively, her rings catching the weak chandelier light, and turned on her heel. "Adds to the vibe. Come on, everyone's waiting."

We followed her out of the foyer and down a wide hallway. The deeper we went, the worse the air got, mold layered over damp wood layered over something else, a smell older and sweeter, like fruit rotting in a closed room.

Maya led us into a large room with high ceilings and a stone fireplace that looked like it hadn't held a fire in years. Soot stains crawled up the chimney breast, and the mantle was cluttered with dead candle stubs and a clock that had stopped at 3:47. The furniture was old, heavy pieces arranged around a worn Persian rug, a room that might have been grand once but had been eaten alive by time.

And there, sprawled across the longest couch like he'd been born on it, was Brian.

My stomach dropped through the floor.

Of all the people in the world. Of all the men Maya could have invited. She'd picked *him*, the one I'd spent two years trying to forget and another three trying to forgive myself for staying with as long as I did. I shot Maya a look that should have burned a hole through her skull, but she was already turned away, pretending to adjust a cushion, pretending she didn't see.

Brian hadn't changed. He was still 6'5" and lean, still carrying himself with that same loose-limbed arrogance, as though every room he walked into owed him something. His hair was shorter, his jaw a little sharper, but the grin was exactly the same, that smug grin men wear when rooms keep rewarding them. Back in college, he'd been the football player everyone orbited around, the one who walked through campus like he was granting the world a favor by existing. I'd fallen for it. I'd been young enough and lonely enough to mistake control for attention, roughness for passion. It took me too long to see what was underneath.

He spotted me the second I walked in. His eyes swept over me — slow, deliberate, a full inventory from my shoes to my face — and the grin spread wider.

"Well, well." He swung his legs off the couch and stood, tugging the hem of his shirt straight. "Look who finally decided to show up." He tilted his head, that same mocking angle he'd perfected in college. "So happy you're here. Single and ready to mingle, right?"

I met his gaze and held it until his grin flickered, just a fraction, just enough. "Not even if you were the last man on earth." I turned away before he could respond, refusing to give him the satisfaction of watching me react. But inside, the old shame was already creeping up my spine, the one Brian had always been able to trigger, the one that made me feel small and foolish and wrong. He knew how to plant it. He'd always known. The sting was designed to linger.

I wouldn't let him see it take root. I couldn't afford to. Not here.

Alex rose from an old ottoman near the fireplace. He'd been sitting so quietly I hadn't noticed him. Which was Alex in a single gesture, always the one observing from the edges, steady and warm and easy to overlook if you weren't paying attention. Back in college he'd been the folklore-and-occult-history one, the guy who could turn a ghost story into a lecture before anyone asked. He met my eyes, and the smile he gave me was the first real thing I'd felt since walking into this house.

Back in college, it had been the three of us, me, Maya, and Alex. Inseparable. I'd always known Alex had feelings for Brian, though he never said it. He wouldn't, not with Brian performing that exhausting alpha act every hour of every day. Brian liked to posture, liked to make sure everyone in the room knew he was the biggest and the loudest. Alex just watched, and waited, and kept the thing he felt locked somewhere behind his ribs.

"Rose." Alex crossed the room and pulled me into a hug, tight and solid, the hug of someone actually glad you're standing in front of them. His chin rested on the top of my head for a second, and I let myself lean into it. "You look great," he murmured near my ear. "I've missed you."

Katie grinned at him from behind me, one eyebrow raised in approval. She didn't know anyone here, but she'd already made her assessment. "Well, at least *someone* around here's got manners." She shot a pointed look at Brian, who pretended not to hear.

My eyes moved to the armchair by the window. Sophie sat folded into it, legs crossed, posture perfect, phone held six inches from her face, her thumbs moving in rapid, irritated taps. She hadn't looked up when we entered. She hadn't acknowledged anyone. The screen's glow lit the underside of her jaw, and her expression was the concentrated scowl of someone losing a battle with their signal.

"Ugh, this place is a dead zone." She jabbed at the screen with her index finger, then flipped the phone sideways, held it up toward the ceiling, and jabbed again. "How am I supposed to post anything?" The question was directed at the room in general, which she still hadn't bothered to look at.

Sophie worked at the same firm as Maya. I'd met her twice, both times at Maya's events, both times briefly. We'd never connected. She existed in a world of filters and hashtags and curated aesthetics, a world where reality was just raw material for content. I didn't dislike her, exactly. I just couldn't find the person underneath all the performance.

She tossed the phone onto the arm of the chair, letting it land with a clatter, and finally lifted her eyes. They swept the room, landed on Maya, and flattened with undisguised displeasure.

"How'd you even find this place, Maya?" The words came out dry and bored, like she was asking about an expired coupon.

Maya's smile stiffened but held. "Some private rental site." She gestured around the room with both hands like a game show host revealing a prize nobody wanted. "No reviews, no host photo. Just a lockbox code from an email that bounced when I tried to reply. But it's supposed to be fun! You know, spooky, thrilling. We all needed a break, right?"

Katie rolled her eyes at me. I gave her a small nod, *I know, I know, just hold on.*

Sophie's gaze drifted from Maya and settled on me. She looked at me for a beat longer than casual, her expression shifting, not hostility, not warmth. A knowing look that said she had information she hadn't decided what to do with yet.

"Oh, Rose." Her tone softened by a single degree. "You're here. I didn't think you'd actually come."

"Why wouldn't I?" I forced the casual into my voice like packing too many clothes into a suitcase. The zipper held, barely.

She watched me for another second, that knowing look flickering, then let it go. But the feeling it left behind didn't go anywhere. She knew something. Maybe she knew everything Maya had done, or maybe it was just an instinct, the sharpness of a woman who spent her life watching people perform and could spot the cracks. Either way, I wasn't ready for that conversation.

I glanced around, suddenly desperate for an exit. "We should get the bags upstairs." The words came out faster than I intended.

Chapter Five

The hallway upstairs was narrow and dim. The wallpaper — some faded floral pattern that might have been green once — peeled at the seams, curling away from the plaster in dry, brittle strips. The floorboards groaned under our feet, each step announcing itself to the house. The ceiling felt too low, the walls too close, and the air had that stale, closed-in quality of a space that hadn't been opened to fresh air in years.

Katie bumped her shoulder against mine as we walked. "You alright?" she whispered, her eyes scanning the hallway.

I gave her the smile, the one that was getting more exercise on this trip than any other muscle in my body. "Yeah, I'm good. Totally fine."

"This place..." She trailed off, her gaze catching on a dark stain on the ceiling, then moving to the shadows pooling at the far end of the corridor. "It's got this weird vibe. You sure we want to stay here? It's creepy as hell."

I shrugged, trying to sound like I believed what I was about to say. "Come on, it's just an old house. Nothing more."

But it didn't feel like nothing. This place crawled beneath the skin. The air sat close, like we were standing inside the house's lungs. I didn't say any of that to Katie. She was already uneasy, and I wasn't about to make it worse.

We wandered the hall, opening doors. A few rooms were already claimed, luggage tossed on beds, toiletry bags on dressers. Brian's, Maya's, Sophie's. There were too many rooms for the number of us, empty ones with unmade beds and the faint smell of mildew, their curtains drawn against whatever light the day still offered.

I caught Brian at the end of the corridor, stepping out of one of the empty rooms. He hadn't heard me. For a second — just one — his face was unguarded. The smirk was gone. The swagger was gone. What was left was a man standing in a dark hallway in a house that smelled like something had died in the walls, and he looked exactly the way the rest of us felt: small. Then he saw me watching. The grin slid back into place so fast it was almost violent, and he cocked his chin at me as he passed, performance restored, audience acknowledged. But I'd seen it. The nothing underneath.

At the end of the hall, I pushed open a heavy wooden door. The hinges screamed, a long, drawn-out creak that traveled down the corridor and died somewhere behind us. My room was large and cold. An old four-poster bed dominated the center, its mattress covered by a dusty quilt in a pattern I couldn't make out through the grime. Heavy curtains blocked the windows, making the room feel more cave than bedroom. A crooked dresser sat against the far wall, its mirror hanging at an angle that reflected a sliver of floor and nothing else, like even the glass had given up trying to show you what was in here.

I tossed my bag near the bed. My fingers grazed the edge of the dresser as I passed it, collecting a layer of dust thick enough to write in.

Katie poked her head through the doorway, her nose wrinkling. "Smells like a tomb in here."

I managed a laugh. It came out thin and hollow, a laugh left out in the weather too long. "Yeah, not exactly five-star. But hey, couple of days, right?"

"Right." She didn't sound convinced. She lingered for a second, then retreated to the room next door. I heard her door click shut, and then I was alone.

I locked the door behind me and leaned against it.

The pressure in my chest was close to unbearable. My breasts ached with pressure, a deep throbbing soreness that radiated into my armpits and down my ribs. I'd pumped before we left Oklahoma, sitting in the kitchen at 5 a.m. while the coffee brewed, but that had been over twelve hours ago and my body was letting me know in the most insistent way possible. Every bump in the road had made it worse. Every seatbelt adjustment. Now, standing still, the fullness pressed outward like something trying to escape.

I pulled my shirt over my head, hoping the release of pressure from the fabric might help. It didn't. The air on my skin was cold and did nothing for the ache. I crouched by my bag and started digging, past clothes, past toiletries, past the extra scarf I'd packed. My hands went through everything twice, then a third time, each pass more frantic.

The pump. I'd left it on the kitchen counter. Back in Oklahoma. Katie had shown up early that morning, knocking while I was still packing, and I'd rushed to get out the door. Grabbed the cooler, grabbed the bags, left the one thing I actually needed sitting next to the coffee maker like a piece of mail I'd deal with later.

I went into the bathroom, small, tiled in cracked white squares, a rust-stained sink and a mirror spotted with age. I leaned over the basin and tried to hand-express, working one breast and then the other, my fingers clumsy and stiff from the long drive. Milk came in reluctant threads that barely eased the pressure. The relief was minimal, like bailing a sinking boat with a teaspoon.

As I worked, a warning prickled across my skin. No board creaked. No shadow moved. Still, my hands stopped. I looked up at the small window above the sink. The glass was clouded with grime, but through it I could see the last gray light of the afternoon, and a shape. Dark. Close.

Wings. The sharp rustle of feathers. A crow, perched on the outside ledge, its head cocked, one black eye pressed close to the glass.

Just a bird. I exhaled through my teeth and went back to expressing. But my hands were less steady now, and the ache barely budged. After ten minutes that felt like thirty, I gave up. I grabbed a fresh bra from my bag, tucked in the nursing pads, and pulled on my loose green co-ords. The fabric skimmed rather than clung, small mercy. I pushed my feet into the soft leather slippers I'd packed, grateful for something between my skin and the cold floors. I draped a scarf around my neck, letting it fall loose enough to cover the damp spots that were already forming.

With a sigh that emptied me, I headed for the stairs.

Downstairs, the living room had transformed from stale to sour. Brian stood at the sideboard pouring wine, that smug grin still plastered across his face, and I noticed the residue before I noticed anything else, white powder dusting the edges of his nostrils, casual as flour on a baker. The table in front of the couch had several lines still laid out, razor-cut and neat, along-side a rolled bill and a small mirror. Maya sat beside the arrangement, legs tucked beneath her, her pupils blown wide and her laughter coming in bursts that were too loud and too fast. She'd joined in. Her energy was manic now, the fake cheer from the front porch cranked to a frequency that made my skin itch.

Sophie sat in the same armchair, phone in hand, her thumb scrolling with the mechanical determination of someone who refused to accept that Wi-Fi didn't exist here.

Brian glanced up as we came down the stairs, and his eyes did what they'd been doing since I arrived, sweeping over me and stopping where they shouldn't. His gaze dropped to my chest, to the scarf draped across it, and the grin stretched wider.

"Well, don't you just look ravishing in this color." His tongue pressed against his bottom lip, a gesture so deliberate it turned my stomach. "Why cover up your assets, Rose?"

My hand tightened around the ends of the scarf, fingers twisting the fabric. "Shut up, Brian."

The grin didn't falter. If anything, it fed, growing fatter off my reaction, off the tightness in my shoulders, the flush climbing my neck. Brian ran on other people's discomfort. Always had.

Katie shot him a glare from behind me — a look that could have cured leather — but didn't spend a single word on him.

I dropped onto the couch. The old cushions gave way beneath me, sinking deep, and I sank with them, too tired to sit upright, too angry to relax. The springs groaned, something dying slowly.

Maya materialized beside me, a glass of wine extended in her hand, that same bright, brittle smile fixed on her face. Her eyes were too wide, glassy from the cocaine, her movements quick and twitchy. She acted like we were at a spa, like she hadn't slept with my husband, like we were still friends who shared wine and told each other everything.

"Let's relax," she chirped, pushing the glass closer to my hand. "We're here to have fun, remember?"

I glanced at the clock on the wall, an old brass thing with Roman numerals, its second hand ticking with a labored, uneven rhythm. "It's nearly six." I shook my head. "No thanks." I set the glass on the side table without looking at her.

Maya's smile stiffened at the edges, a hairline crack in the performance, there and gone. She pulled her phone from her pocket, tapped the screen, and music spilled from a portable speaker somewhere behind the couch. Music with a heavy bass line, too loud for the room, too festive for the mood. Without missing a beat, she stood and started swaying her hips. Slow at first, then wider, more exaggerated, like she was putting on a show for an audience that hadn't asked for one.

Brian was up in seconds. His hands found her waist, fingers spreading wide, settling into the curves like they belonged there. Maya's movements shifted, more suggestive now, her body pressing back against his, her hips rolling in slow, deliberate circles. It wasn't dancing. It was a performance, the kind designed to make everyone in the room either watch or leave.

My stomach turned. The sight of them together, his hands on her hips, her back arched against his chest, that performative, Look-at-me energy radiating off both of them, sent a wave of nausea through me. *Maybe that's how she did it,* I thought, watching Maya grind against Brian's thigh, her head tipped back, her throat exposed. *Maybe that's how she got to Phoenix.* The thought was acid. I swallowed it before it burned through.

"I'm gonna check out the place." I stood up fast, almost knocking the wine glass off the side table.

Katie was on her feet before I finished the sentence. "Yeah, let's go explore. I've seen enough of this show." Her voice was flat, disgusted, already moving toward the door.

Alex nodded and fell in behind us. Even Sophie had reached her limit. She pushed herself out of the armchair with a groan, pocketing her phone.

"Better than watching *that.*" Sophie jerked her chin toward Maya and Brian. Maya had both arms around his neck now, practically in his lap, while Brian leaned back with the self-satisfied look of a man who believed the world existed for his entertainment. "I think I just lost my appetite for the rest of the trip."

For once, I agreed with her completely. I turned toward the foyer and kept walking, the others falling into step behind me. The sound of the music and Maya's breathless laughter faded as we moved through the house, replaced, slowly, by the groaning of old wood, the draft whistling through unseen gaps, and the heavy, watchful silence of a building that had been empty for far too long.

Chapter Six

Together, we stepped outside.

The overgrown fields stretched before us, wide and wild and forgotten. The grass had grown past any reasonable height. Waist-high in places, thick and coarse, left to grow unchecked for years until it became a dense, hostile thicket. It brushed against our legs as we waded into it, dry stalks scratching at our clothes, and beneath our feet the ground was uneven, pitted with hidden dips and the stumps of things that had been cut down long ago. The air out here was different from the stale rot inside, colder, sharper, carrying damp earth and an older sweetness, like vegetation left to decay in standing water.

Sophie kicked at a clump of grass, her shoe sending up a spray of dead seed heads. "This place is so boring." She shoved her hands into her jacket pockets, her shoulders hunched up around her ears. "I could've been at a party, but instead I'm stuck here for Halloween. What the hell was Maya thinking? How is this supposed to be fun?"

I gave a short, nervous laugh, automatic, hollow, my body

filling a silence my brain hadn't caught up with. "You know Maya. She likes to push boundaries, even when no one else cares."

We walked past an old barn set back from the main house, maybe fifty yards out. Its roof had caved in on one side, the beams snapped and hanging at angles, the remaining shingles dark with moisture and rot. Ivy had climbed every surface it could reach, thick, woody vines crawling up the walls and threading through the gaps in the siding, pulling the structure into the earth one season at a time. The barn was being eaten alive, slowly, patiently, and it had stopped fighting back a long time ago.

Alex paused beside it, running his hand along one of the rusted tools still hanging from a nail on the exterior wall. A sickle, its blade orange with corrosion, its wooden handle split and gray. His fingers lingered on the metal for a moment, his brow creasing. "Look at this place," he murmured, pulling his hand back and wiping the rust on his jeans. "It's like no one's touched it in years."

I glanced at the trees ringing the field. They were old. Lifetimes old, their age cut into every furrow of bark. Their trunks were twisted, and their branches reached outward and upward in gnarled, arthritic arrangements that looked less like growth and more like grasping. Skeletal fingers, I thought, and immediately wished I hadn't. Their shadows smeared across the uneven ground and shifted when the wind moved through the canopy, making every patch of shade feel unstable, like it might slide toward you if you looked away.

The whole property had the feeling of a place that had been left alone, not peacefully, not the way a garden rests in winter. Aggressively, as though the world had turned its back and the land had taken offense. It wasn't dead. That was the unsettling thing. It was alive in the wrong ways. Growing where it shouldn't, decaying where it should have held, and underneath all of it, a waiting quality. A held breath.

I turned around.

Behind us, the mansion loomed against the gray sky, its silhouette all wrong angles and sagging lines. The windows were black, not dark, black. Empty sockets in a face made of stone and rotting wood. I couldn't shake the feeling they were aimed at us, aimed, deliberately, with intention.

I turned back to the field, fast. I didn't want to look at those windows anymore.

The tall grass swallowed me as I stepped ahead of the others, the stalks closing in on either side, brushing my arms, my hips. It was a maze built by something that didn't want you to find the center. The others' voices faded behind me — Sophie's complaint, Alex's murmured response — growing muffled and distant as the grass rose higher.

And then I stopped.

It was right there. Ten feet ahead, mounted on a crooked wooden post driven into the earth.

A scarecrow.

The clothes were the first thing I noticed, tattered flannel shirt, the fabric faded and ripped, lifting in the low wind with the indifference of something that had long since stopped fighting the weather. But beneath the clothes, the body was wrong. A normal scarecrow sags. This one held shape. Shoulders with width. A torso with weight. The proportions were too close to real, too close to human, and the wrongness of it made my eyes try to slide away even as my brain kept pulling them back.

Half the head was covered by a burlap sack, loosely stitched with dark thread that crossed the fabric in uneven, puckered seams. Below the sack, the lower face was exposed. And below that, leather pants. Leather pants clung to its legs, cracked and weathered but unmistakably deliberate. Who dresses a scarecrow in leather pants?

But it was the mouth that held me.

Open. Cracked like old leather left in the sun. The lips — if you could call them lips — were stretched into a crooked, lopsided smile that pulled wider on one side than the other, exposing a dark gap where the teeth would be. The skin around the mouth was textured wrong, too detailed, too creased, each crack individual and precise, as though something once alive and supple had dried into this frozen expression over time.

It looked disturbingly, unmistakably human.

"That thing's creepy as hell." Sophie's voice came from right behind me, and I nearly left my body.

"God — " I pressed a hand to my chest, the air knocked clean out of me. "You scared me."

Sophie laughed, the sound bright and unexpected against the heavy air, and for a second the tension broke. Katie and Alex caught up and joined in, relieved laughter, the laughter that comes because something is wrong and laughing is easier than admitting it.

Sophie bent and picked up a long stick from the ground. She jabbed the scarecrow in the midsection with it, giggling as the figure swayed on its post, the tattered shirt flapping. "Perfect for Halloween, though." She poked it again, harder, and the whole frame rocked.

I couldn't tear my eyes away from the mouth. That smile. It was wider than it should be, and the more I looked at it the less it looked like something carved or constructed and the more it looked like something that had been alive once and dried into this expression on its way out.

"Leave it alone," I muttered, the words coming out harder than I intended.

Sophie looked at me, one eyebrow raised, then shrugged and dropped the stick. It landed in the grass with a soft thud. "Alright, buzzkill."

We walked on. But I kept glancing back. Every few steps, my head turned on its own, checking. The scarecrow shrank behind us as we moved deeper into the field, its shape growing smaller, but that crooked smile stayed the same size in my mind. Fixed, unchanging, as though it had burned itself onto the back of my eyelids.

Katie touched my arm, a gentle squeeze, just enough pressure to pull me back. I managed a smile and felt a little steadier. But my body didn't agree. My skin was still prickling, the fine hairs on my arms still raised, and somewhere in the base of my skull, something was quietly insisting that we shouldn't have come out here.

Deeper into the field we found a well, half-swallowed by vines. The stones were old, hand-cut, furred with black moss. I leaned over the edge. The water sat far below, the color of old tea, and my face came back to me from the surface. Distorted, the features stretched into something I almost didn't recognize as mine.

After a while, Sophie stepped back, wiping her palms on her jeans. "Let's head back." The boredom in her tone was thinner now, stretched over something she wasn't willing to name.

Katie nodded, already turning. But I didn't move.

"You guys go ahead." The words came out firm. More certain than I felt. "I just need a minute."

Katie stopped mid-turn, her brow creasing. "Are you sure? We'll wait—"

I shook my head. "I'm fine. Just need a minute."

She searched my face for a beat, looking for something that would justify overriding me, then relented. She nodded once — reluctant, unhappy about it — and the three of them started back through the grass, their shapes shrinking, their voices fading until I couldn't hear them anymore.

I was alone.

I stared into the well, and the well stared back, and inside my head the same names circled like water finding a drain.

Phoenix. Maya. The lies. The photos on the phone. His shrug. Her smile. The hospital bed. The envelope. All of it spiraling, tightening, pulling toward a center I couldn't quite reach. I was supposed to be planning the confrontation, rehearsing the words, sharpening the delivery, figuring out when and where to corner Maya and force her to see what she'd done. But standing here, alone in a dead field with my hands on the stones of a forgotten well, all I could feel was the anger coiling and recoiling inside me, a snake eating its own tail, going nowhere.

I clenched my fists against the stone until my knuckles ached.

A sound — sudden, loud, close — snapped the spiral in half.

Flapping. Wings beat somewhere above me, like canvas caught in a gale, but lower, thicker, with a weight behind it that canvas doesn't have. The sound filled the air around me, sourceless and everywhere.

I spun around, the skin on the back of my neck tightening. I scanned the sky, the gray, fading expanse of it, the treeline, the spaces between the branches. Nothing. The sound stopped as abruptly as it had started.

The light was going. The gray afternoon had thinned to a pale, washed-out dusk, and the shadows from the trees had stretched so far they'd merged with each other, turning the field into a patchwork of dark and darker. I needed to get back.

I pushed away from the well and started walking.

Each step sent a sharp ache through my breasts. The pressure had built past discomfort into an ache that had crossed from discomfort into urgency, a deep, throbbing fullness that radiated with every movement. The nursing pads were soaked through, the moisture spreading beyond them into the fabric of my bra, and I could feel the dampness on my skin, warm and uncomfortable. I gritted my teeth and kept moving, my stride quickening.

Halfway back, or what I thought was halfway, it was hard to tell with the grass this high and the light this low, the frustration boiled over. I reached inside my shirt, fingers hooking the edge of one pad and then the other, and yanked them both out. They were heavy in my hand, saturated, useless. I tossed them onto the ground without breaking stride, without looking back.

A mistake I wouldn't understand until later.

I kept my head down, focused on the uneven ground, my arms wrapped around myself against the chill that had crept in with the fading light. When I finally looked up, I stopped dead.

The scarecrow. Right in front of me. On its post. I'd taken the wrong path through the grass and walked straight back to it.

In the dusk, it was worse. Everything that had been unsettling in daylight was grotesque now. The burlap sack looked darker, the stitching sharper, and the exposed mouth — that frozen, crooked smile — seemed wider than before. More open. More eager. The leather pants caught the last gray light and gleamed dully, wet-looking.

I swallowed. The sound was too loud in the quiet. My pulse throbbed in my ears, a thick, rapid drumming that seemed to sync with a rhythm I couldn't place, a rhythm in the air, a frequency just below hearing.

Walk past it. Don't stop. Don't look.

But my feet had other plans. A pull took hold of me. Not a hand. Not a force. A compulsion that started in the center of my chest and drew me forward one step at a time. It had found the pads. It had tasted the milk. Now the hook was in me, tugging from somewhere below thought, as though whatever had tasted me had earned the right to call me closer. I didn't want to go. Every rational part of my brain was screaming to turn around, to find a different path, to run. But my legs kept moving, steady and sure, as if they'd been given instructions I hadn't approved.

I stopped inches away. Close enough to smell it, damp fabric, earth, and organic warmth that didn't belong on a scarecrow.

My hand came up. I watched it rise like it belonged to someone else. My fingers extended, trembling, and touched its leg. Just below the knee. A light press, barely more than a brush of fingertips against the surface.

Under the fabric, it wasn't straw. It wasn't rough or dry or hollow.

It was warm. Solid. Dense and yielding in the way that flesh yields, muscle beneath skin, unmistakable, alive.

I snatched my hand back. My throat closed. Bile surged and I swallowed it down, the acid burning all the way.

This isn't right. This isn't—

And then the scarecrow breathed.

It was slow. Deliberate. An inhale that went on too long, lifting the chest beneath the tattered shirt, swelling the torso outward, the burlap sack on its head shifting with the movement as air was drawn in. Drawn from the space around me, pulling at my hair, my clothes, the grass at my feet, as though the breath was large enough to take everything near it inside.

I stumbled backward. My heel caught in the grass and I staggered, arms pinwheeling, a choked sound escaping my throat that was too strangled to be a scream.

No. No no no no—

I turned and ran.

The grass whipped at my legs, the stalks slashing at my calves, my thighs, stinging like thin blades. My breath came in ragged, tearing gasps, each one burning my throat and never filling my lungs. Behind me — above me — around me, the sound returned. Wings. Not the papery flutter of birds. Heavier. With weight and span and muscle behind each stroke. The air displaced by each beat pressed against my back like a hand.

I didn't look up. I couldn't. I just ran, blind, frantic, my left slipper lost somewhere in the grass, my bare foot hitting the raw earth with every stride, every root and stone a threat, every shadow a shape.

A darkness passed over me. Fast. So fast it was more of a sensation than a sight, a pressure drop, a cooling of the air, a shadow that moved against the direction of the remaining light. Close. Too close. Right above me.

My legs pumped harder. My arms swung. My lungs screamed. The house. I could see the house, the dark shape of it against the sky, and if I could just reach it, if I could just—

My foot struck something hard — a rock, a root, I never knew — and the ground came up to meet me with sudden, absolute violence. I went down face-first, the impact slamming the air out of my chest and filling my mouth with the taste of dirt and blood. My hands hit the earth palms-down, the skin tearing, and my forehead bounced against the hard ground with a crack that turned the world white for a second.

I didn't get up.

I couldn't.

I lay there, face pressed into the earth soaked cold through my shirt, and I squeezed my eyes shut as tight as they'd go. As if not seeing could make it not real, as if the dark behind my eyelids was safer than the dark that was above me, around me, closing in.

A wet breath moved over me.

Close. Right against the side of my neck. I felt the displacement of air — warm, moist, rhythmic — passing over my skin, my hair, my ear. The sniffing was deliberate, methodical. Not the quick, darting investigation of an animal. Slower. Methodical. Taking its time. Learning me. The sound moved from my neck to my shoulder, down my arm, back up to my jaw. Each pass sent a wave of ice through my blood.

It pulled back. The warmth withdrew. For one second, I believed it was leaving. That it was done. That it had decided I wasn't what it wanted.

Then it came back.

I forced myself to look. Not a decision, a compulsion. My lashes parted, just a fraction, just enough to see through the narrow slit between my eyelids.

And my insides turned to water.

The creature crouched over me, massive and wrong and too close. It wasn't the scarecrow anymore, not really, yet it wore the scarecrow's shape like a snake wears old skin, loosely, temporarily, something to be shed when it was no longer useful. The tattered shirt hung off shoulders that were too broad, too muscled, too *real*. The burlap sack had slipped to one side, revealing the contour of a skull that wasn't quite human. The proportions off, the angles too sharp, the shadows pooling in places they shouldn't. And the eyes —*God, the eyes* — were gold. Gold — not yellow, nothing like amber — the color of metal pulled from a furnace and still cooling. They burned in that half-hidden face with an intelligence that made my stomach drop through the earth.

In one hand, it held my breast pad.

I watched — unable to breathe, unable to close my eyes again — as its fingers tightened around the saturated pad. Milk seeped between its fingers, white against the gray of its skin. It brought the pad to its cracked mouth and squeezed. The milk fell in a thin stream, landing on its tongue, and the gold in its eyes darkened. The color pulled back like a tide, the bright molten center swallowed by a blacker hunger. Its eyes rolled back. A sound came from deep in its chest, not a growl, not a moan. A sound between the two. It vibrated through the ground beneath me and into my bones.

It was *savoring* it.

I shut my eyes. I couldn't look. The wrongness of it, the intimacy, the hunger, the grotesque tenderness of those massive hands squeezing milk from a pad meant for a baby that never existed. It broke something in my ability to process. My mind went blank, a screen of static, and all that was left was the animal terror flooding every nerve.

Then I felt it.

Cold. Wet. A sensation dragging across my face, slow, rough, deliberate. A tongue. Wide and textured, moving from my jaw to my cheekbone in one long, unhurried stroke. Not tasting me the way a predator tastes prey. Tasting me the way something *savors*. Like I was the first real thing it had tasted in a very long time.

My mouth opened. The scream built in my chest, climbed my throat, reached my lips—

And the world went black.

Chapter Seven

When I came to, I was on a sofa.

The room arrived in pieces, sound first, then light, then the dull, persistent ache at the back of my skull that pulsed with each heartbeat. Voices drifted around me, distant and formless, a conversation heard through a wall. Someone was talking, maybe laughing. The cushions beneath me were old and soft, sinking under my weight in a way that made it hard to tell where the sofa ended and I began.

I was caught between sleep and waking. That disorienting limbo where you know something is wrong but can't remember what, where the body is trying to come back online and the mind is dragging its heels because it knows what's waiting on the other side. The fire was crackling somewhere to my left. The air smelled like smoke and stale wine and the underlying must of the house that had settled into everything.

"You're awake." Brian's voice cut through the fog before anything else could. I blinked — my eyelids heavy, gummed together — and his face swam into focus. He was leaning over me, arms folded across his chest, that smirk already set in place, waiting for me to open my eyes. "You were heavy as hell to carry in here with Alex." He tilted his head, letting the comment land, his lips twitching. "Thought we'd need a forklift."

I groaned and pushed myself upright. My arms trembled with the effort. My head had been packed with wet sand, dense, throbbing, every pulse of blood pushing against the inside of my skull. The room tilted, steadied, tilted again. I blinked until things sharpened.

Alex stood a few feet from the sofa, his body angled toward me, his weight shifted forward on the balls of his feet, the posture of someone ready to move. His face was tight with concern, brow creased, his eyes tracking me with the careful attention of a person waiting for bad news. Katie hovered just behind him, her hands twisting together in front of her stomach, fingers knotting and unknotting in a restless cycle. She was chewing the inside of her cheek. Something she did when she was trying not to cry.

Maya sat further back, curled into the corner of the opposite sofa with her wine glass resting on her knee. The glass caught the firelight in a thin amber line along its rim. Her face was hard to read in the low light, but her posture was deliberate, relaxed, legs crossed, head tilted at an angle that said *I'm watching but I'm not worried.* Sophie was beside her, arms folded, her expression neutral in a way that felt studied.

"What happened?" Katie's voice was soft, careful, the voice you use with someone in a hospital bed. Her fingers stilled against each other, her eyes searching my face.

I swallowed. My throat was raw, parched, scraped, as if I'd been breathing through my mouth for hours. My brain scrambled to organize the fragments: the field, the dusk, the scarecrow on its post. The breath. That inhale. Deliberate. Enormous. The chase through the grass, the fall, the face-down impact with the cold earth. And then — above me, over me — the sniffing, the breast pad in its hand, the milk squeezed between its fingers. The tongue. Cold and wet and slow, dragging across my face like it was mapping the geography of my skin.

My stomach lurched at the memory. I pressed the back of my hand against my mouth.

"Something..." I started. My voice came out hoarse, splintered. I tried again. "Something chased me in the field." I swallowed against the tightness in my throat. "I think it was the scarecrow."

Brian broke it first. He snorted — a sharp, nasal sound, dismissive and loud — and leaned back against the arm of the couch, one leg crossing over the other. His eyes were too bright, the pupils dilated, the cocaine still circulating and making everything he said come out faster, harder, meaner.

"A scarecrow. Really?" He drew the words out, each syllable soaked in sarcasm, his head shaking slowly. "Losing it, aren't you? This is getting sad, Rose." He paused, let the words settle, then raised both eyebrows in mock concern. "Did it come to life and try to steal your soul, too?"

"Brian, shut up." Alex's voice snapped through the room like a branch breaking. He dropped to a crouch beside me, his knees hitting the floor, and his hand found mine, gripping it, squeezing, anchoring me. His eyes were level with mine, steady and searching. "Are you alright now?" he asked, his tone low enough that it was meant only for me.

I nodded, though my body disagreed. I was still shaking, a fine, involuntary tremor running through my arms and legs, and my pulse was doing something erratic that I could feel in my fingertips.

Before I could say anything else, Brian's laugh filled the room, the performative kind, the kind designed to establish the official story before anyone else could offer an alternative.

"Oh, come on." He spread his hands, palms up, appealing to the room like a lawyer making his closing argument. "It's a freaking scarecrow. Rose probably tripped over her own feet and passed out." He looked at me, his grin sharpening. "All this stress is getting to you, huh? The divorce, the... everything?" He waved a hand vaguely in my direction, encompassing the entirety of my life with a single lazy gesture.

Maya shifted in her corner of the sofa, her wine glass tilting as she brought it to her lips. She took a slow sip, watching me over the rim, and when she lowered it, her mouth was set in a smirk that she probably thought looked sympathetic. "Really, Rose?" Her tone was the verbal equivalent of a pat on the head. "You're running from scarecrows now?"

My fingers curled into the sofa cushion, nails digging into the worn fabric. The anger came up hot and fast, punching through the fog of pain and confusion. "I'm serious." My voice came out louder than I expected, sharp, cracked at the edges. "There was something there, Maya. A shape in the field. It chased me. I'm not making this up."

Sophie unfolded her arms and stood. She didn't say anything. She crossed the room toward me, her steps measured, and stopped a few feet away. The look she gave me wasn't cruel. It wasn't mocking, like Brian's. It was worse in a way I couldn't immediately name. It was the look of someone who had already drawn their conclusion and was now simply waiting for you to catch up. A look that said: *I hear you. I just don't believe you.*

"I'm not crazy." The words came out of me before I could shape them. Defensive, hot, flushed with the humiliation of saying something true to people who have already decided it isn't. "I know what I saw. I know what I felt."

"Of course you did," Brian murmured. He exchanged a glance with Maya, quick, conspiratorial, the shared look of two people who had agreed on a version of events. He leaned forward, his forearms resting on his knees, that smug expression spreading across his face like something he couldn't contain. The cocaine was making him bolder than usual, sharpening the cruelty that he normally kept just below the surface.

"Let's be real, Rose." His tone dropped, not softer, just lower, more deliberate. He was enjoying this, settling into it like a cat into a warm spot. "You've got a lot going on. Phoenix, the divorce..." He counted them off on his fingers, casual, like reading a grocery list. "It explains a lot." He paused, and I could feel what was coming before he said it. The air in the room changed — thickened — and I saw Katie stiffen beside me.

"And you're still not over your kid." The words came out smooth, unbothered, as if he were commenting on the weather. "I mean, you're still..." His eyes dropped. Slowly. Deliberately. Down from my face to my chest, and the look that crossed his features was a look caught between amusement and disgust. "Lactating."

The word landed in the room, a stone dropped in a pond.

I looked down. The scarf around my neck had shifted when I was carried inside — pulled loose, bunched to one side — and the damp spots on my shirt were fully visible. Two dark, spreading circles over each breast, unmistakable, exposed for everyone to see. My body, the thing I'd been trying to hide, the thing I was ashamed of, the thing that still produced milk for a baby who would never drink it, was on display.

Brian's eyes stayed on my chest for a beat too long, then lifted to my face. His grin was back, wider now, feeding on the moment. "Stress can do weird things to people."

"Brian!" Katie's voice cracked through the room, sharp and furious. She took a step toward him, her hands balling into fists at her sides, her mouth set in a hard line. "What the hell is wrong with you?"

He held up his hands. Palms out, the universal gesture of *what did I say?*, but the grin didn't move. He shrugged, one shoulder lifting and dropping with the boneless ease of someone who had never once been held accountable for the things that came out of his mouth.

I stared at him. The anger burned through the humiliation and came out the other side as resolve. "Maya told you all of that, didn't she?" The words came out through clenched teeth. "About Phoenix. About the baby. She handed you my life like a party trick, and you just loved it."

Brian's smirk twitched, a micro-flinch, there and gone. He recovered fast, tilting his chin up. "People talk, Rose. It's not my fault your life's a mess."

But I'd seen the flinch. That was answer enough.

I sat there. The humiliation was a physical thing. Hot across my cheeks, tight in my throat, pressing down on my chest like a weight I couldn't shift. The memory of the field, the creature's breath on my skin, the tongue, the breast pad squeezed between those massive fingers, collided with the reality of this room. These people. These faces staring at me with varying shades of pity and contempt.

"I swear I'm telling the truth." But even to my own ears, the words sounded thin. Shaky. The kind of declaration that undermines itself by needing to be made at all. The memory of that tongue, cold, rough, dragging across my face like I was something to be tasted and catalogued, made my skin crawl. I wanted to scrub my face until the sensation disappeared. But they didn't believe me.

Not one of them.

Katie moved closer. Her hand came to rest on my arm. Gentle, warm, the careful pressure of someone trying to hold you together without admitting they think you might be falling apart.

"Rose." Her voice was soft. Measured. The tone she used when she was trying very hard to be kind about something unkind. "Maybe it's just everything piling up." She paused, choosing her words carefully, testing each one like footing on ice. "We had a really long journey. Your body's exhausted, you forgot the pump, you're in pain, that's real. All of that is real." She squeezed my arm. "Maybe you just need to rest."

She meant well. I knew she meant well. Katie was the last person in this room who would hurt me on purpose. But I could hear it — underneath the gentleness, threaded through the careful phrasing — doubt. She wanted to believe me. She was trying. But the wanting wasn't the same as the believing, and the gap between them was wide enough to fall through.

I pulled my arm away from her hand. Not roughly, just a withdrawal, a closing. The frustration bubbled up through the humiliation, mixing with the fear and the anger until I couldn't tell which was which anymore.

"I'm not imagining this," I whispered.

But my voice was too small, and the room was too big, and nobody heard me.

Or if they did, they chose not to.

I sat on that sofa, surrounded by people, and I had never been more alone in my life. The fire crackled. Brian poured himself another drink. Maya swirled her wine. Katie stood beside me with her hand hovering near my shoulder, not quite touching, not quite pulling away.

And somewhere outside, in the dark field beyond the black windows, the thing from the field was breathing. It had tasted me. It knew my scent, the salt of my skin, and the exact composition of the milk leaking through my shirt.

I knew it wasn't over. Even if they didn't.

Chapter Eight

The room went dark.

The lights died in one clean instant, as though a hand inside the walls had yanked the current out by its roots. The fire still crackled in the grate, throwing orange light in a rough circle that reached the nearest couch and stopped, leaving everything beyond it in solid black. The shift was so sudden that my eyes cramped, pupils straining to adjust, and for two full seconds nobody moved.

Then everyone grabbed their phones.

Six screens lit up at once, their bluish glow carving hard shadows on startled faces. The flashlights worked. Nothing else did, every screen showed the same dead bars, the same useless spinning wheel where signal should have been. Brian swept his phone in a wide arc, the beam bouncing off portraits and doorframes. Maya clutched hers against her chest, the light pointing upward and turning her face ghoulish, all cheekbones and hollow eye sockets.

Maya let out a small laugh. It was supposed to sound

casual, but the pitch was wrong, too high, too quick, a sound that tripped over its own feet. "Well, that's... spooky."

Brian swung his beam toward me, the light hitting my face and making me squint. "Nice going, Rose." He pointed at me with his free hand, his grin twitching at the corners, nerves dressed up as bravado. "You keep talking about creepy stuff, and now we're stuck in a haunted mansion with no lights." He spread his arms wide, performing for the room. "Guess you jinxed it! This just keeps getting better."

Alex was already on his feet, his phone held low, the beam angled at the floor. His face was half-lit and calm, the controlled calm of someone who had decided to be useful while everyone else was busy being loud.

"It's probably just the fuse." His tone stayed steady and practical. "I'll check the main switch in the basement."

The word *basement* landed in the room and sat there, ugly and unwanted. A pause followed, the kind where everyone suddenly has somewhere else to look. Then the excuses arrived, one after the other, overlapping like dominoes falling.

Brian shifted his weight from one foot to the other, his free hand finding the back of his neck. "Yeah... no." He attempted a chuckle that came out thin. "Basements are creepy, man. Especially in places like this." His eyes darted toward the hallway that led to the basement stairs, then away. Quick, involuntary, the movement of a man who didn't want to admit what he was afraid of.

Maya set her wine glass on the side table with a careful clink, her fingers lingering on the stem. "You're brave, Alex, but I don't think I'd be much help down there." She gave an apologetic smile that was mostly teeth. "Electrical stuff? Not my thing."

Sophie, who had been off her phone since the signal died, pulled her jacket tighter across her chest. "I'd come, but..." She trailed off, her nose wrinkling. "Basements. Dark. Spiders." She held up her palms. "Not really my scene." Her tone was lighter than the others, not mocking, just honest. She knew her limits and wasn't pretending otherwise.

Katie sat on the edge of the couch, her knees pressed together, her teeth working her bottom lip. "I'm kind of terrified of the dark." Her voice was soft, not ashamed, just truthful. "And basements." She shrugged, her shoulders tight against her ears. "Sorry."

Alex sighed through his nose, the exhale long and measured. A muscle in his cheek flexed once, frustration held on a short leash. "Alright, fine. I'll go by myself."

I stood up.

The last place on earth I wanted to be was underneath this house. My body was still humming with the aftershock of the field — the creature's breath on my neck, the tongue, the blackout — and the thought of descending into the dark belly of this mansion made my stomach clench so hard I tasted bile. But Alex was going down there, and he was going alone, and I couldn't let that happen. Not after what I'd seen, knowing what I knew.

"I'll come with you." The words came out steadier than I felt. My legs were trembling, but I locked my knees and kept my face still.

Katie looked up at me, her eyes wide in the phone light. "Rose, are you sure? After everything..."

I nodded. The motion was for myself as much as for her. "Yeah. I'll be fine." I didn't believe it. But some things have to be done whether you believe in them or not.

73

Katie hesitated — one beat, two — then stood. She squared her shoulders, her hands balling into fists at her sides, the gesture of someone forcing their body into courage it didn't naturally possess. "Well, if you're going, I'm not staying here." A small, tight smile crossed her face. "Strength in numbers, right?"

"Right." Alex returned the smile, and I could see the relief break across his features, subtle but real, the easing of tension around his eyes. "Let's just get this over with."

Brian aimed his phone beam toward the hallway that led to the basement door, the light carving a narrow path through the dark. "Good luck, guys." His voice was pitched to sound careless, but his free hand had found his thigh and was gripping the fabric of his pants. "Don't get eaten by the house or anything."

The hallway was worse in the dark.

Every detail that had been merely unsettling in daylight was menacing now. The peeling wallpaper curled away from the walls in dry, crackling strips that caught the phone light and threw strange shadows. The floorboards protested every step, groaning now, deep wooden sounds that vibrated up through the soles of my feet. And beneath the groaning, beneath our breathing and the whisper of our clothes as we moved, there was something else. A feeling more than a sound. The sensation of attention, of being observed by something that had no eyes but didn't need them.

We'd walked this hallway earlier in the daylight. It had been old, dusty, unremarkable. Now, in the dark, it had become a different space entirely. Longer than I remembered, narrower, the ceiling lower. The dark compressed everything, squeezed the dimensions until the walls felt close enough to touch without extending my arms.

The basement door waited at the end.

When we reached it, a draft hit us, cold enough to sting, pushing through the gap at the bottom of the door with enough force to stir the dust on the floorboards. It didn't smell like old air. It smelled like earth. Earth from too far below the house, the kind you find when you dig past the topsoil into the layer that hasn't seen light in decades. Beneath it was a sweet organic rot, like overripe fruit. Or meat left too long in a warm room.

Alex, Katie, and I stood there, shoulder to shoulder, our phone lights aimed at the door. Nobody moved. Nobody volunteered to go first. The draft kept pushing, cold and insistent, as if something on the other side was exhaling.

When it became clear that waiting wasn't going to make it easier, I reached forward and turned the handle.

The door swung inward with a low groan, and the dark below was —*absolute black*— a black that had texture, that pressed against your open eyes and makes you doubt whether they're working at all. The stairs descended into it and vanished, each step visible for a few feet in our phone beams before being swallowed by the void.

Katie made a sound. Small, involuntary, slipping out before she could catch it. "Damn." She swallowed hard, her throat clicking. "Do we really have to go down there?"

"It's the only way." My forehead was damp, sweat beading along my hairline despite the cold. I could feel it sliding toward my temples. My voice sounded braver than my body felt, and I was grateful for the discrepancy.

We descended.

The cold increased with each step, layer by layer, each step down pulling us through air that had been sitting cold and sealed for years. By the time we reached the bottom, the air was sharp enough to sting the inside of my nose with each breath.

Our phone beams swept the space. The basement was larger than I'd expected, wider, deeper, the ceiling higher than made sense for a space beneath a house. Shelves lined the walls, bowed beneath rotting cardboard boxes and mason jars clouded with age. Thick dust coated everything in a gray, undisturbed layer that hadn't been touched in years. Maybe decades. The floor was hard-packed dirt, cold through the soles of my feet, and the air tasted stale and mineral, the taste of licking stone.

We fanned out, moving slowly, our beams crossing and diverging as we searched. The silence down here was different from the silence upstairs, heavier, more complete, as though the basement existed in its own acoustic world, sealed off from everything above. The sounds of the house — the settling, the creaking, the wind against the windows — didn't reach. Down here, there was only our breathing and the soft scuff of our steps on dirt.

Alex found the fuse box first. His beam caught the edge of a gray metal panel mounted on the far wall, spotted with rust, its door hanging slightly ajar. He crossed to it, and Katie and I followed, our lights converging on the box.

He pulled the panel open. Inside, the mechanism was old. Not the modern circuit breakers I was used to, with their neat rows of labeled switches. This was a manual system, a single heavy switch mounted on a ceramic base, requiring a deliberate physical motion to operate. No automatic tripping. No overload protection. You turned it on by hand, and you turned it off by hand.

And it had been turned off.

The switch sat in the down position, firmly, cleanly, not the halfway position of something that had been jarred loose or tripped by a power surge. It had been pulled down. Deliberately. With intent.

"Someone did this," I whispered. The words fogged in the cold air.

Katie's fingers closed around my forearm, her grip tightening until I could feel each individual finger through my sleeve. "But why would—"

I didn't wait for her to finish. I reached up, curled my fingers around the switch, and shoved it up, the mechanism resisting for a second before giving with a heavy, metallic *chunk.*

The lights above us sputtered to life. A harsh, electric buzz filled the stairwell as the fluorescents in the hallway upstairs flickered on, their glow spilling down the first few steps. For a moment, relief washed through me, before sense could stop it, at the simple fact of artificial light existing again.

But the relief died fast.

The light reached the top of the stairs and stopped. It pooled on the upper landing, lit the hallway beyond the door, illuminated the peeling wallpaper and the dusty floorboards, and went no further. The basement remained exactly as dark as it had been. The bulb above us stayed dead, intact but lifeless in the ceiling, the filament simply refusing. The house had power again. The basement wouldn't take it. Our phone beams were still the only light down here, and the contrast made the darkness feel denser, more deliberate. In the thick, subterranean black, a thing had drawn a line and said *no further.*

Katie's nose wrinkled, her nostrils flaring. "God, this place stinks." She waved her free hand in front of her face, her fingers fanning the air. "Let's get out of here."

She was right. The smell had worsened since the lights came on upstairs, the change in current stirring something, disturbing a pocket of trapped air. It was stronger now: that sweet, organic undertone had intensified into something unmistakable. Rot. Decay. The smell of things that had stopped being alive a long time ago but hadn't finished decomposing.

We turned toward the stairs. We were done.

And then Alex's flashlight swept across the far wall and caught something we hadn't seen.

A door.

It was in the farthest corner of the basement, half-hidden behind a collapsed shelf and a stack of water-damaged crates. Heavy, wooden, set into the stone wall with iron hinges that had turned black with oxidation. The wood itself was old — ancient — the grain visible even under the grime, the surface scarred and dark.

"Wait —" Alex's beam steadied on the door. He tilted his head, his body going still. "What's that?" He held up a hand, palm out, signaling us to be quiet. "Do you hear that?"

I heard it.

Flies. The sound was faint but insistent, a buzzing that came from behind the door, muffled by the wood but unmistakable. Not the lazy drone of a few insects caught in a windowsill. This was dense, layered, the sound of many flies in a confined space, their wings beating against each other in a constant, humming swarm.

I couldn't move. My feet had rooted to the dirt floor, and my body was caught between the urge to run and the compulsion to know. Alex started toward the door, his steps slow and careful, his flashlight leading. Katie and I stayed where we were, too frightened to follow, too frozen to leave.

My beam drifted as I shifted my weight, the light sliding across the dirt floor, and it caught something. A shape, half-buried in the packed earth, one corner protruding at an angle.

I crouched without thinking about it, my fingers brushing the dirt away. The grime was cold and damp, gritty under my nails. Beneath it was a book bound in cracked leather, darkened by age and moisture.

I worked it free from the dirt, my fingers trembling. It was heavier than it looked, dense, solid, the covers warped and swollen from years of ground moisture. The leather was tooled with symbols I didn't recognize, pressed into the surface in patterns that seemed to shift when I tilted it under the light.

"Alex." My voice was thin and unsteady. It was all I could manage. "Look at this."

Alex stopped — he'd been halfway to the door — and came back. His brow furrowed as he took the book from my hands, turning it over, his thumbs brushing the cover. He cracked it open. The pages were brittle, yellowed to the color of old bone, and they crackled when he turned them. Strange symbols covered every page, hand-drawn, precise, in ink that had faded to a reddish-brown that made me think of things other than ink. Foreign text ran alongside the symbols in dense, cramped script.

The color drained from his face. I watched it happen, a visible paling, the blood withdrawing from his skin as his eyes moved across the pages. His hands started to shake. Not a tremor. A shake, starting deep and working its way outward until his whole arm was involved.

"What is it?" I could barely form the words.

Alex swallowed. His Adam's apple bobbed once, hard. "It says *Codex Arcanum*." His voice had dropped to something just above a breath, low, tight, strained in a way I'd never heard from him. "It's black magic, Rose. The real thing." He looked up from the pages, and the fear in his eyes was exposed, unguarded. "I've studied fragments like this in my master's work, but I don't know if I'm translating it right. Half of this is damaged. I never thought I'd hold one." He ran his thumb along the edge of a page, the paper whispering against his skin.

Katie had backed up a full step. Her face had gone the color of skim milk, her lips pressed into a thin line that was barely holding. "We shouldn't be here," she muttered, shaking her head. "We should not be here. Let's just get out."

"Yeah, but the door — " Alex gestured toward it with the book still clutched in his hand. "Check the door."

"No." Katie's voice shook, but the word was hard. Definitive. "We are not checking it."

But my feet were already moving. I didn't tell them to. They just went, carrying me toward the door the same way they'd carried me toward the scarecrow in the field, as if some part of my body understood a compulsion my mind hadn't agreed to. Alex fell into step beside me, the book pressed against his chest.

The door was thick, three inches of solid wood, aged to the color of charcoal. The smell was stronger here, seeping through the gaps around the frame like something alive, pushing its way out. I raised my phone and angled the beam across the surface, squinting at the marks carved into the wood. They were shallow, worn smooth by time, but still legible, letters, cut into the grain with a blade.

"*Creatura Noctis,*" I whispered. The Latin felt old on my tongue, carrying a weight that had nothing to do with the phonetics and everything to do with what the words meant.

Alex leaned close, his breath clouding in the cold air. His eyes traced the same letters, his lips moving soundlessly. "*Creature of the night,*" he translated. He stared at the words, his jaw working. "It sounds familiar, like I've read it some-where—"

He opened the book. His fingers moved through the pages with urgent, trembling speed, scanning symbols and text until they stopped — suddenly, completely — on a page near the middle. The same words were there, hand-lettered at the top of the page in larger script: *Creatura Noctis.*

Below the heading, dense paragraphs of text ran alongside illustrations, several figures rendered in dark ink. The same creature drawn in different shapes: a winged thing crouched on a rooftop, a shadow stretched across a field, something with a man's silhouette standing in a doorway. Shape-shifter. I looked away from the faces. They were wrong in ways I couldn't hold in my mind long enough to describe.

Alex's mouth had gone dry. I could hear it in the way his lips stuck together when he spoke. "It says..." He traced a line of text with his finger, translating in halting phrases. "It feeds on humans... once a year. During the darkest night." His finger moved down the page. "Before nightfall, it can stir. It can scent. It can mark. But it cannot fully feed until the house goes dark." His finger stopped. His eyes lifted to mine. "They call it the Creeper."

He turned another page, scanning, then stopped. "This part I can read. It says the creature can be killed by — " He blinked. His face went hard with concentration. "By fire. By

81

destroying its dwelling before the feeding is complete." He looked up at me, a grim certainty in his eyes. "That's our way out, Rose. If we can trap it and burn this place down."

He was wrong about that. I didn't know it yet. But he was wrong. Alex had translated it wrong. Fire killed the dwelling, not the thing the dwelling caged.

The name dropped into the cold air between us and stayed there, heavy as a stone at the bottom of a well. My blood went cold, not a figure of speech, not a metaphor. I felt the temperature of my body drop, felt the chill push outward from my core to my fingertips, my toes, the roots of my hair.

Katie spun on her heel. Her shoe scraped against the dirt floor, and she was on the first step before either of us could speak.

"I'm leaving." Her voice cracked down the middle, half command, half sob. "I didn't sign up for this shit."

Alex and I turned to follow. And that's when our phone lights swept across the walls.

We'd missed it on the way down. In the dark, with our beams focused on the floor and the fuse box, we hadn't looked up. Hadn't looked at the walls themselves. But now — with the stairwell lit from above and our phones angled wider — we saw it.

Claw marks.

Deep, gouging claw marks, raked across the plaster in long, savage strokes. Grooves, not scratches, three and four inches deep in places, torn through the plaster and into the lath beneath, the wood splintered and pulled outward as though something had dragged its claws through the wall with tremendous force and no hesitation. They covered the walls on both sides of the stairway, dozens of marks, layered over each other, some old and gray, some newer, the exposed wood still pale.

And they were smeared with blood.

The blood had dried to rust-brown flakes at the edges, but it was unmistakable. The marks weren't random. They were frantic. Desperate. The marks of something — or someone — clawing at the walls while being dragged.

My legs gave out for a second, my knee buckling before I caught myself on the railing. My breath came in fast, shallow hitches that I couldn't control.

"Guys!" Katie's voice came from above, high, breaking, teetering on the edge of tears. "Don't be stupid! Hurry up!"

"She's right." Alex's face was gray. He grabbed my hand — his palm was slick with sweat, his fingers colder than the basement air — and pulled me toward the stairs. The book fell from his other hand, hitting the dirt floor with a dull thud, and he didn't stop to pick it up. Didn't even look back.

We took the stairs two at a time. My foot slipped once on the worn edge of a step and Alex's grip tightened, wrenching my arm, keeping me upright. We burst through the basement door and slammed it behind us, the wood shuddering in its frame, the sound cracking through the hallway like a gunshot.

I pressed my back against the door. My chest was heaving. My pulse was beating so hard and so fast that the edges of my vision had gone gray, and for a second I thought I was going to pass out again. The fluorescent light above us hummed its steady, mindless hum, and the hallway stretched in both directions — normal, lit, ordinary — but nothing about it felt safe.

Because I knew. With a certainty that had settled into my bones like ice water, I knew that whatever was behind that door, whatever had carved those marks into the walls, whatever fed once a year on the darkest night, whatever they called the Creeper. It wasn't going to stay down there.

It was coming up.

Katie leaned against the opposite wall, her forehead pressed against the plaster, her shoulders shaking. She lifted her head, and her face was streaked with tears she hadn't bothered to wipe. Her breath came in ragged, uneven gasps.

"We need to tell the others," she managed. The words were barely held together, cracking at every seam.

We did. We really did.

Chapter Nine

Katie, Alex, and I stumbled into the living room, the cold of the basement still pressed into our clothes, our skin, our lungs. My breath came in rough, uneven bursts, and I could feel the tremor running through my arms, something deeper than adrenaline, something the warmth of the upstairs couldn't touch. The claw marks were still behind my eyes. Every time I blinked, I saw them, those desperate, gouging streaks, layered over each other, smeared with old blood.

Brian didn't even look up.

He was pouring wine at the sideboard, his back half-turned to us, the bottle tilted at a lazy angle. His posture said everything before his mouth did: this was theater, and we were the entertainment.

"Let me guess." He set the bottle down and turned, that smirk already in place, polished and ready. His eyes swept over the three of us — disheveled, pale, breathing too hard — and his lips twitched with amusement. "Rose saw another ghost?" He tilted his head. "Maybe the scarecrow moved again?"

Alex stepped forward, his chest still heaving, one hand raised. "Brian, listen—"

But Brian talked over him, his voice rolling out to smother whatever came next. "Blood, symbols, and what, flies now?" He barked a laugh, short, harsh, designed to establish the room's temperature before anyone else could. "Jesus, Rose. What are you trying to sell this time? You sound insane."

Maya sat beside him on the arm of the couch, her wine glass balanced on her knee, one leg crossed over the other. She giggled at Brian's performance — a cocaine-bright, jittery sound, too loud and too fast — her eyes glassy and wide. "First the scarecrow, now this?" She tilted her glass toward me, a gesture that was half-toast, half-dismissal. "Maybe you should sit down before it gets worse."

My fists clenched at my sides, the nails pressing crescent moons into my palms. I forced my breath to slow. "We found a door." I tried to keep my tone level, trying to sound like someone worth listening to. "Behind it, there were flies, hundreds of them, buzzing. And the smell..." I shook my head, swallowing against the bile that rose at the memory. "Something's wrong down there."

Brian rolled his eyes. A slow, exaggerated rotation that he held for a beat too long, making sure everyone caught it. "Yeah, *wrong*." He dropped air quotes around the word with his fingers. "Old houses smell bad, Rose. That's how it works."

Katie's voice broke through, unsteady but pushing forward. "There's more." She gripped the back of the nearest chair, her knuckles pale against the dark wood. "We found a book. Some kind of... evil book. Ancient. With symbols and rituals." She looked around the room, searching for a single face that was taking this seriously. "This place isn't normal."

Maya sighed, a long, theatrical exhale that collapsed her shoulders and tilted her head back. "You mean like a grimoire or something?" She brought her wine to her lips, took a slow sip, and lowered it. "Seriously? All three of you sound like you're off your meds."

A thread snapped.

The break inside me was quiet, a thread pulled past its limit, the last millimeter of give used up. I felt it go in the center of my chest, and what rushed through was rage. Pure, white-hot rage built over months — over years — compressed and stored and denied until this exact moment.

"Enough!" My voice cracked through the room, louder than I intended, raw-edged and trembling. Everyone went still. "You think I *want* this? There's blood on the walls down there, dried blood, smeared across claw marks deep enough to put your fingers in. And someone turned off the power on purpose. That switch didn't trip. It was pulled. Deliberately."

Brian sat up straighter, his grin twitching, not fading yet, though the muscles around it were working harder to hold it in place. The cocaine was still running his system, sharpening everything, stripping the insulation from every impulse. He leaned forward, forearms on his thighs, and locked his eyes on mine.

"Always a story with you, Rose." His tone had dropped, lower, stripped of performance, aiming. "Always something falling apart." He counted on his fingers, ticking off my life, a list of defects. "First, I was the abusive one in college." One finger. "Then Phoenix was the cheater." Two fingers. "Now it's a scarecrow and a smelly basement." Three fingers. He wiggled them. "Do you even hear yourself? You're pathetic."

The word hit me where it always hit me, in the soft place between my ribs where every man who had ever diminished me had learned to aim. But this time, it didn't land the way he expected. This time, the impact didn't collapse me. It ignited me.

"Wow, Brian." I stepped forward, closing the distance between us by half. My voice was steady now, low, controlled, sharp as a surgical instrument. "You're still hung up on the college thing?" I held his gaze and didn't blink. "You *were* abusive. That's not a story. That's a fact." I took another step. "Phoenix *was* cheating. Also a fact." Another step. "And yeah, the scarecrow moved, and the basement is weird as hell. And you can sit there counting on your fingers all night, but it doesn't change any of it."

Alex stood behind me, frozen. I could feel his tension without turning around, the rigid posture, the quick breathing, the internal war between wanting to back me up and wilting under the force of Brian's presence. Brian had always had that effect on Alex, making him smaller just by occupying the same room.

I didn't wait for backup. I stepped closer to Brian, close enough to see the faint white residue still dusting his nostrils, close enough to watch his pupils dilate. "There's something down there, Brian. Something real." I hit every word like a nail being driven. "But go ahead, keep laughing."

For a second — just a second — the smirk faltered. Then it was back, wider than before, forced into place by an ego that couldn't afford to let it slip.

Maya uncrossed her legs and leaned forward, her wine

glass dangling from her fingers. A cruel, practiced smile spread across her face, the smile of someone who had learned that the best defense was a targeted, personal demolition.

"Brian's right, you know." She let the words drip, each one placed with precision. "It's a fact. You always need something to fall apart over." She tilted her head, studying me the way you'd study something mildly disappointing. "Maybe you're the problem, Rose."

Sophie shifted in the doorway, her arms still crossed, and when she spoke, her tone was quiet. Almost casual, like she was observing something obvious that everyone else had missed. "Maya told me about Phoenix, you know." She glanced at Maya, then back at me. "She thought the whole thing was hilarious."

The room compressed.

Everything I had buried, every sleepless night, every sob I'd choked down at 4 a.m. with the pump humming beside me, every time I'd looked in the mirror and seen the woman Phoenix had thrown away, every text from Maya that I'd read and re-read knowing the smile behind it was a lie. It all rose at once. A year's worth of grief and fury and humiliation, ascending through my body, something volcanic and unstoppable, burning everything it touched on the way up.

I lunged.

My hands found Maya's face before I registered moving, fingers curling, nails sinking into the skin along her jaw, digging in. I felt the flesh give under my grip, felt the ridges of her cheekbone beneath my palm. "You bitch — " The words tore out of me, cracked and molten. "You've got some NERVE!"

Her wine glass slipped from her fingers and snapped

against the floor, the sound swallowed by the chaos. Red wine spread across the old wood like a stain. Brian jumped to his feet, his hands coming up. "Rose, what the hell—!"

Maya recoiled, her hands flying to her face. My nails had left tracks, three thin lines across her left cheek, already beading with blood. Her eyes were wide, her mouth open, shock fracturing the performance she'd maintained since we arrived. For one second, the mask was gone. And underneath it, she was just a woman who hadn't expected to get hit.

She recovered fast. Her hand pressed against the scratches, blood smearing between her fingers, and her mouth twisted into something between a snarl and a sneer. "Rose, you're insane—"

"You slept with my husband!" The scream ripped out of me with enough force to scrape my throat raw. I could feel the tears and the fury competing for my face, both of them winning. "You cheating, sniveling, low-life whore!"

The room went silent. The crackling fire. The drip of wine from the table's edge. The faint buzzing of the lights overhead. That was all.

Maya's face changed, not crumbling, not breaking. Hardening. Her jaw set. Her bloodied hand dropped to her side, and she squared her shoulders, pulling herself up to her full height. When she spoke, her voice was different, stripped of the playfulness, the teasing, the performance. What was underneath was defensive, cornered, venomous.

"You think *I'm* the reason?" She jabbed a finger toward me, her hand trembling. "Phoenix was done with you long before I came along." Her words came faster, sharper, a woman throwing punches with her mouth because her fists weren't enough. "You were too much, Rose. Too needy. Too emotional. Too everything. He was suffocating, and you couldn't see it because you were too busy clinging—"

"Stop."

I didn't shout it. I said it, low, flat, with a calm that surprised even me. The word cut through Maya's monologue, a blade through ribbon, and she stopped. She went quiet because the temperature of my voice had changed, and something in her recognized it.

I leaned forward with control. My eyes stayed on hers.

"You'll never be more than a side piece, Maya." Each word was measured, placed, precise. "For Phoenix. For Brian. For every man you've thrown yourself at." I watched her face and saw the first hairline cracks appear behind her expression, in the structure that held it up. "They all use you, and then they toss you aside. You're a good time. That's all you've ever been." I paused for a moment to memorize the shock on her face and then spoke again. "None of them ever wanted more. None of them ever put a ring on your finger, did they?"

Maya's mouth opened. Nothing came out. Her lips moved — the beginning of a word, a defense, a comeback — but it died on her tongue. For the first time since I'd known her, she had nothing. The cracks were spreading, and she couldn't stop them.

Brian, still standing, still reeling from the explosion he'd helped detonate, lifted his hands in a placating gesture. "Alright, maybe we should all just—"

"Shut up, Brian." I didn't look at him. My eyes stayed on Maya for one more beat — watching the cracks — and then I turned.

His smugness was still there, but it was thinner now, a film over something less certain. He straightened, chin lifting, the reflex of a man who responded to challenge by making himself bigger.

"You want to keep running your mouth, Brian?" I squared my shoulders, my chest still heaving. "Because the only thing smaller than your brain is your dick."

I turned to the others. Katie, Alex, Sophie, all of them staring, all of them still. "Yeah." I pitched it loud enough for the walls to hear. "Brian could never get past second base because he was too ashamed of his size. First time he showed me? I laughed." I watched Brian's face. The smirk was gone. In its place was something I'd never seen there before. Stripped of his usual armor, a man stripped of the only armor he had. "And after that, he got nasty with me. So I had to dump him."

Brian's mouth opened. Closed. His mouth worked, the muscles bunching under his skin, but whatever he was trying to say couldn't find its way out. His hands had dropped to his sides, fingers twitching. The room was looking at him the way he'd spent the whole trip looking at me. And he couldn't handle it.

Katie's hand closed around my arm, firm and anchoring. "Rose." Her voice was steady now, not gentle, not careful. Steady. "None of this matters right now. Let's get out of here."

I took a breath. Then another. The rage was still in me — I could feel it circling, hot and restless — but the worst of it had been spent. The weight I'd been carrying — the unsaid things, the swallowed fury, the months of pretending — was lighter. Not gone. But lighter, like I'd set down a suitcase I'd been dragging up a hill.

"Yeah, let's go." Alex spoke from behind me, the words cracking the tension like a stone through glass.

The three of us turned toward the foyer.

Chapter Ten

And that's when the sound began.

It started distant, far below, muffled by the floors and walls between us and the basement. A breaking sound. A cascade of glass, then wood, then something heavier. Stone. The sounds layered over each other, building, multiplying, and with each second they grew louder, closer, as if whatever was making them was climbing through the house toward us.

Everyone froze.

The noise became frantic. It was everywhere now, in the walls, in the floors, the vibrations running through the soles of my feet and up into my legs. The old chandelier overhead began to sway, its crystals clinking together in a high, chattering melody that had no business being beautiful in a moment this terrifying.

Maya's face had gone white. "What the hell is that?" She backed away from the center of the room, her bloodied hand pressed against her mouth.

Katie's complexion matched the plaster. "What is happening?" She grabbed my arm, her fingers digging in, her eyes locked on mine. Searching for an answer I didn't have.

Then, a different sound. Wings.

This was nothing like the papery flutter from the field or the distant flapping I'd heard at the well. Each beat moved the curtains, stirred the dust, and pressed against my eardrums hard enough to make my teeth ache. The rhythm was deep and slow, a sound that belonged to nothing that flew in the natural world. It vibrated through the floorboards, through the walls, through the marrow of my bones.

We bolted.

The six of us — me, Katie, Alex, Brian, Maya, Sophie — all of us ran. No discussion, no hesitation, no one leading. Pure animal instinct, herd-panic, legs moving before brains could organize a plan. We poured out of the living room and into the foyer, feet slipping on the dusty floor, arms pumping, breath ragged.

A blur of darkness shot over our heads.

I ducked on instinct, my shoulders hunching, my hands flying up to cover my skull. The shape was massive, a shadow made solid, too fast to see clearly, too close to ignore. The displaced air hit me like a shove, and the sound of it — the rush, the muscular force of wings cutting through space — was deafening, a roar of displaced atmosphere that swallowed every other sound in the room.

It landed.

The impact shook the floor. I felt it through my feet, through my knees, in the base of my spine. A heavy, deliberate *thud* that cracked the old tile and sent a spider-web of fractures radiating outward from the point of contact. The creature stood between us and the front door, and for the first time, I saw it clearly.

His wings opened first, but they did not look made for sky. The membranes were gray-green and scarred with old tears. Along the lower edges, tiny barbs hooked and unhooked, pale as fishbones, each one moving on its own.

His body followed: long arms, too many knuckled joints, grayish-green skin stretched over ribs that moved in a shallow double rhythm. Black veins branched under the surface like ink poured into meat. His hands hung low beside his thighs, each claw curved inward and wet at the tip.

Then the face.

It was almost human, which made it worse. The jaw looked built to unhinge. Thin seams ran from the corners of his mouth toward his ears, the skin puckered there like old stitches. His eyes burned gold beneath a ridged brow, and when he breathed, the air carried damp earth and iron.

The mouth stayed closed. Waiting.

His eyes swept the room. The gold came when he wanted. The black came when he hunted.

Brian was closest. His shoulders lifted, pure habit, the old reflex to make himself bigger. His hands ruined it. They shook at his sides, fingers jerking in small spasms he could not hide.

Sophie pressed both hands over her mouth. Maya slipped behind Brian. Somewhere beside the fireplace, Alex had gone very still.

Katie broke last. Tears slid down her face without sound. One hand found my sleeve and closed there, hard enough to twist the fabric. She could not stop looking at him.

Then his gaze found me.

The foyer receded. The people. The fear in every body around me. It left only us in a space that felt smaller and hotter than any room should be. Hunger moved behind those eyes, threaded with curiosity and recognition. His pupils dilated, the gold irises narrowing to thin, glowing rings around expanding black centers.

His gaze dropped to my chest.

He studied the damp stains on my shirt, the shape of my breasts beneath the fabric. His nostrils flared. Recognition moved across his face, quick and awful, as if the rest of the room had gone flat and I was the only thing left with blood in it.

A grin spread across his face. Slow. Deliberate. The corners of his mouth pulling up and back, revealing the edges of teeth that were too sharp, too numerous, too white against the gray of his skin. He inhaled again — deeper this time, his chest expanding, his eyes half-closing — and the grin stretched wider.

The lips parted. A tongue slid out, forked at the tip. It moved through the air between us and tasted me without touching. The sight sent a jolt low through my body, and I hated myself before I even understood why.

Sophie screamed.

The sound was a blade, sharp, piercing, slicing through the charged air between the creature and me with enough force to shatter the moment like glass dropped on stone. Her hands flew to her mouth a second too late, the scream already out, already echoing off the walls, already filling every corner of the foyer with the raw, animal sound of someone who had reached the end of what their body could contain.

The Creeper's head snapped toward her.

The grin vanished. What replaced it was something older,

something that lived beneath the almost-human features, predatory, stripped of everything except function. His wings snapped open, the membranes pulling taut, their span blocking the light behind him. For one frozen instant, he was a silhouette, massive, winged, the shape of something that belonged in the dark spaces of old paintings, in the margins of illuminated manuscripts, in the nightmares of people who had been dead for centuries.

Then he moved.

The speed was wrong. Not fast the way a person is fast, or an animal, nothing that obeyed the physics of muscle and momentum. He *blurred*, a dark smear crossing the space between where he stood and where Sophie was pressed against the wall, the distance eaten in a fraction of a second, the air popping in his wake.

His clawed hand clamped over her mouth. The impact drove her head back against the wall, the plaster cracking behind her skull. Her scream died to a muffled, keening sound behind his palm, her eyes bulging, her hands clawing at his wrist, fingernails scraping uselessly against skin that didn't give.

He lifted her. One hand. Her feet left the floor, her body dangling, her legs kicking in frantic, useless arcs. She weighed nothing to him. She *was* nothing to him.

His other hand drew back. The claws extended, five curved points, each one the length of a finger, gleaming dully in the firelight. For one second, he held the pose — Sophie suspended, his claws poised — and the deliberateness of it was the worst part. He wasn't rushing. He was *showing* us.

The claws plunged into her abdomen.

The sound was something I would hear for the rest of my

life. Wet. Thick. A tearing, parting sound that had no equivalent in any experience I'd had before or wanted to have again. Sophie's body convulsed, a single, violent spasm that arched her back and snapped her head forward. Blood erupted from the wound, *spraying*, thick, dark, arterial, splattering across the floor and up the walls in long, fanning arcs.

Her muffled screams turned to choking, gurgling, liquid sounds that bubbled from behind his clamped hand. Blood spilled from the corners of her mouth, running down her chin, dripping onto his wrist.

He ripped his claws upward.

The motion was savage, a single, wrenching pull that split her torso from navel to sternum. Her body opened. What was inside came out in a rush I couldn't look at and couldn't look away from. The stench hit a second later, iron and bile and something animal and familiar that my brain recognized before my conscious mind could process it. The smell of a body that was no longer a body.

He released her. She dropped. The sound of her hitting the floor was small for the violence that had preceded it. A dull, wet thud, and then stillness. She lay in a spreading pool of dark red, her eyes open, her face frozen in the last expression it would ever hold.

The Creeper turned back to us.

Blood hit the floor one drop at a time, soft, metronomic taps. His chest rose and fell with steady, unhurried breaths. And across his face — that knife-cut face — a smile spread, not a grin or a snarl. A *smile*. The smile of something deeply, profoundly satisfied, looking at its audience and daring them to do something about it.

We ran.

I didn't decide to run. My legs decided. Every survival circuit in my body fired at once, and I was moving before my brain could form the thought, my feet pounding the old floorboards, my arms pumping, my breath a raw, tearing sound in my throat. Behind me — above me — the sound of wings. Massive, rhythmic, each beat pushing air downward with enough force to lift the dust from the floor and press against my back like a hand.

Katie stumbled beside me — her foot catching on the edge of a rug, her body lurching forward — but she caught herself, her hands slapping the wall, and she kept moving. Alex was ahead of us, his legs churning, his face a mask of blind determination. He reached the door at the end of the hallway first — a heavy wooden door with an iron handle — and wrenched it open with both hands.

We tumbled through. Bodies colliding, tripping, grabbing at each other and the doorframe. Brian and Maya were somewhere behind us — I heard them, heard their footsteps and their ragged breathing — but I didn't look back. I couldn't look back.

Alex slammed the door shut. The impact shook the frame, sent dust sifting from the ceiling. Hands fumbled at the lock — his hands, my hands, someone's hands — and the bolt slid home with a metallic *clack* that echoed through the narrow space.

Then we just breathed. And looked at each other.

Brian was the first to move. He crossed to the window — the tall, narrow one facing the front of the house — and tried to wrench it open. It didn't budge. He swore and shoved harder, the muscles in his forearms standing out, his breath hissing through his teeth. Then he stopped. His hands fell to his sides.

"The window's boarded." Every trace of performance had left him. "From the outside. Planks and bolts."

Alex checked the next window. Same. Thick wooden planks crisscrossed the glass, bolted from the wrong side. Katie tried a side door that should have led to a service corridor. Dead-bolted. The bolt was on the outside — the *outside*— as though someone had walked through this house and sealed every exit from the exterior, one by one, with the calm precision of a person locking a cage.

"Every way out," Alex whispered. His palm pressed flat against the boarded window, his fingers spread. "All of them. Sealed from the wrong side."

I looked toward the front window, the one that should have shown the driveway, the gravel, the Honda. Through a gap between the planks, I pressed my face close to the glass and looked out.

The driveway was gone. Where gravel had been, there was only grass, wild, thick, overgrown, as if no road had ever existed. The trees had closed in, their branches knitted together where the road should have cut through. The house had swallowed the way out.

I stepped back. My legs felt like they'd been hollowed out and filled with sand.

Sophie's face — open eyes, frozen mouth, the blood — hung in the dark behind my eyelids. I pressed my back against the wall and slid down until I was sitting on the cold floor, my knees drawn up, my head bowed. The image wouldn't leave. The sound wouldn't leave.

Some things, once they get inside you, never come back out.

Chapter Eleven

The adrenaline was still buzzing through me, a chemical hum in my blood that made my fingers tingle and my teeth ache. Every muscle in my body had drawn tight, locked in the position they'd assumed during the sprint, and they hadn't gotten the message that we'd stopped moving. My legs shook. My teeth were clenched so hard I could feel it in my skull.

Katie had slumped against the wall, her back pressed flat against the plaster, her knees buckling until she slid halfway to the floor. Her face was the color of wet paper, her hair plastered to her forehead with sweat, her chest rising and falling in rapid, shallow hitches that didn't seem to bring enough air. She stared at the locked door, her mouth slightly open, and I wasn't sure she was seeing it.

Alex had retreated to the far corner. He stood with his back against the wall and his hands braced on his thighs, bent forward at the waist like a man about to be sick. His eyes were open — too wide, the whites visible all the way around — and they kept moving: door, window, door, window, door. A loop he couldn't break.

Brian paced the length of the room in long, rigid strides, his path covering the same six feet over and over. His fists were balled at his sides, and under his breath he was muttering, curses, fragments, nothing coherent. The cocaine was still in his system, sharpening every edge, stripping away the buffer between stimulus and reaction. Each time he reached the wall, he'd spin on his heel and come back, the turn tight and angry, a caged animal working a track into the floor.

Maya stood in the center of the room, arms locked around her own body so tightly the tendons in her forearms stood out like cords, not pacing, not sitting, barely breathing. She was holding herself together. Literally. Her breath came in thin, rapid sips, and her eyes — wide, glassy, rimmed with smeared mascara — stared at nothing. The scratches on her cheek from my nails were still beading, three thin red lines that she hadn't bothered to wipe.

"What the hell was that thing?" The whisper came from Maya, so quiet I almost didn't catch it. Her lips barely moved. She turned her head toward me, slow, the motion stiff, as though her neck had rusted. "Was that the thing you saw in the fields?"

I nodded. The motion was small. My body didn't have the energy for more.

Her eyes widened, not the performative shock she'd been selling since the front porch, but something unguarded and bare. Her hand came up to her mouth, pressing against her lips. "Oh my god."

The room held that for a moment. Five people and a silence that was full of things none of us wanted to say.

Alex straightened. He pushed himself off the wall and stood by the locked door, one hand resting against the frame, needing the contact to stay upright. The color hadn't returned to his face. His lips were dry, cracked at the corners, and when he spoke, his voice was barely there, a sound pushed through a throat that had forgotten how to make noise at normal volume.

"It's the Creeper."

Brian stopped pacing. His head snapped toward Alex, nostrils flaring. "Spit it out, Alex. What the hell is that creature?"

Alex ran a trembling hand through his hair, the fingers catching in the tangles, pulling. His throat worked for a second before the words found their way out. "The Creeper. I recognized the name from the Codex. And from a seminar I took. It was supposed to be folklore." His eyes lifted and met mine, and what I saw in them wasn't academic detachment. It was the look of someone who had studied the legend and was now standing inside it. "But this..."

He trailed off. His gaze drifted to the door, to the thing on the other side of it, and the sentence died.

"They say the Creeper is something ancient," he continued, his voice dropping lower, each word dragged out reluctantly, as though speaking it aloud made it more real. "Born from blackness, the oldest darkness, the darkness that existed before anything else. He comes every Halloween, when the night is at its thickest." He paused. Licked his lips. "He doesn't just take bodies. He feeds on fear. On life itself. Drains everything from his victims and leaves..." Another pause, longer this time. "Leaves nothing but empty shells."

Maya's hand dropped from her mouth. Her chin dipped, her eyes losing focus as the meaning of Alex's words settled into her. "Fed off them?" The question was barely more than a shape, lips moving, air passing through, but the sound itself had been hollowed out by the terror running through every syllable.

I forced myself to speak. My voice came out wrong. Smaller than I wanted, thinner, a voice that belonged to someone standing at the edge of something she couldn't come back from. "We have to get out of here."

My eyes darted to the window. It was the one exit we hadn't tried. A tall, grimy pane set into the far wall, the glass so coated with years of dirt that it had turned from transparent to translucent, the world outside reduced to a vague gray smear.

"The window." I pushed the words out. "Try the window."

Katie nodded fast, and we moved. All of us. A scrambling, graceless rush toward the one thing that might still be an exit. Alex got there first. His hands found the edges of the frame, fingers digging into the gap between wood and sill, and he pulled. His knuckles went white. The tendons in his forearms stood out. His face twisted with effort.

"It's stuck!" His voice cracked, splitting down the middle. He shifted his grip, yanked harder, his feet bracing against the baseboard. The frame creaked — a low, straining sound — but it didn't move. "It won't budge!"

Brian shouldered Alex aside. He planted his hands on the frame and pulled with his full weight, his body leaning back, legs locked. The wood groaned, resisted, held. He cursed — a sharp, barked word — and pulled again, harder. Nothing.

Then we saw why.

On the other side of the glass, visible through the grime as dark horizontal bars, thick wooden planks crisscrossed the window. Three of them, weathered planks crossed the window, secured with bolts driven through the wood and into the surrounding masonry. Not nailed. *Bolted.* The kind of permanent, deliberate reinforcement that took tools and time and intention.

Someone had sealed this window shut. Not from the inside. From the *outside.*

The realization hit me in the gut. Whoever had been here before us, whoever had sealed these windows, whoever had hidden the book and carved the warning into the basement door. They hadn't been trying to keep something out.

They'd been trying to keep something in.

Brian spun around. His face was a battlefield, rage and terror fighting for control, neither winning, both visible. His chest heaved, his breath coming in sharp, serrated bursts, and when he spoke, his voice rose with every word, climbing toward a register he couldn't sustain.

"What the hell is this place?" His arm shot out, his finger stabbing toward Maya. "What did you bring us to?"

Maya flinched. The motion was small but visible, a tightening of her shoulders, a pulling-back of her chin, the involuntary reflex of someone bracing for a blow. For a second — half a second — guilt crossed her face. I saw it. A flicker in her eyes, a softening at the corners of her mouth, the ghost of something that might have been remorse. Then she buried it. Her face reset. Her spine straightened. And when she spoke, her voice was shaking but defiant.

"I didn't know!" Both hands came up, palms out, fingers spread. "It was supposed to be a surprise! A break." She swallowed, and her eyes flicked to me. Quick, involuntary, weighted with something I couldn't name. "For Rose. I felt guilty, and I wanted to do something for her."

The words landed and burned.

A break. For me. Because she *felt guilty.*

"A pity party?" My voice came out raw, scraped hollow. I stared at her, and I could feel the disbelief reshaping my face, pulling my eyebrows up, dropping my jaw, twisting my mouth into something that wanted to laugh and scream at the same time. "You felt guilty for screwing my husband, and *this* is what you came up with?" I gestured around the room. The boarded window, the locked door, the blood I could still smell from the hallway. "I didn't ask for your guilt, Maya. I didn't ask for any of this!"

Maya's lip trembled. She started to respond, her mouth opening. But whatever she was going to say was swallowed by the sound.

The wings.

Slow. Deliberate. Each beat heavy enough to feel through the floorboards, through the soles of my feet, up into my ankles. The rhythm was unhurried — measured, patient — the pace of something that had all the time in the world and knew it. The sound grew louder with each beat, closer, filling the room from the walls inward until I could feel it pressing against my eardrums.

The temperature dropped.

Not gradually. It fell, a sudden, biting cold that arrived all at once, as if someone had opened a door to January. I could see my breath. My arms broke out in gooseflesh, every hair standing upright. The cold settled into my bones, into the spaces between my joints, and it brought a heaviness with it, a dread that had physical mass, that pressed down on my chest and made each breath a labor.

Katie whimpered beside me. A small, involuntary sound, high and thin, pushed out between clenched teeth. Her breath came in shaking clouds, and her whole body was vibrating with a tremor she couldn't control. I gripped her arm. My fingers dug in. I wasn't sure if I was steadying her or anchoring myself.

Brian's fear had turned. The panic was still there, in his darting eyes, in the sweat at his temples, in the way his chest pumped. But it had curdled into desperation, selfish and sharp.

"We can't just sit here waiting for that thing to come for us!" His eyes swung toward me. His arm came up, one finger pointed at my chest, and the accusation was already loaded before the words arrived. "It looked at *her.*" The finger jabbed. "It wanted Rose." His gaze swept the room, searching for allies, for anyone who would agree. "Maybe... if we give him what he wants..."

Nobody spoke. Nobody moved. The wing-beats continued their slow, approaching rhythm, and in the gap between Brian's words and what came next, I heard my own heartbeat and hated that it was still working.

Katie's head snapped up. Her eyes, which had been glazed and distant, came into sharp, blazing focus, the unfocused terror burned away by something hotter and more immediate. Her teeth clenched, the muscles bunching along her jaw, and when she spoke, her voice was shaking but fierce.

"Are you out of your mind?" She stepped forward, one short, aggressive step that brought her close enough to Brian to make him lean back. "You're just going to sacrifice her? Throw her to that thing to save your own pathetic ass?"

Brian held his hands up, palms out, the gesture of a man trying to talk his way out of a corner he'd backed himself into. His expression was desperate, the performance of reasonableness applied to something unreasonable. "Look, I'm just saying — " His tongue darted over his lips. "We all saw it. He was... drooling over her. Maybe if we give him Rose, the rest of us—"

The room tilted. Not literally — the floor stayed where it was, the walls held their shape — but something inside me shifted, some internal gyroscope that kept the world level and comprehensible. Brian would feed me to that creature. He'd hand me over like a peace offering, like a meal, like something disposable. And he'd do it without a second of hesitation if it meant saving his own skin.

But that wasn't the worst part.

The worst part was Maya.

She said nothing. She stood there — arms limp at her sides, her face carefully, deliberately blank — and said nothing. No objection. No protest. No "Brian, stop." Just silence. And in that silence, I heard everything she wasn't saying.

She was calculating. Weighing it. Deciding whether Brian's suggestion had merit.

Then she moved.

Maya stepped forward from the middle of the room, and her face changed. The hard, defensive mask she'd been wearing since I'd scratched her cheek softened, slowly, deliberately, like wax warming. Her eyes glistened, tears welling along her lower lids, catching the dim light. Her lips parted, trembling.

"No." The word came out as a whisper, cracked and raw. She shook her head, her hair swinging. "Brian's wrong." She took another step, closing the distance between us. Her voice dropped lower, thicker, weighted with emotion. "Rose... I've hurt you enough." A tear spilled down her uninjured cheek, cutting a dark line through her foundation. "I'm so sorry. For Phoenix. For everything."

She reached me. Her arms opened, and then they were around me, pulling me in, wrapping tight, her body pressing against mine. She was warm. Shaking. Her tears fell onto my shoulder, soaking through the fabric. Her breath hitched against my neck in ragged, broken rhythms.

"I never meant for it to go this far," she whispered. The words were muffled against my shoulder, spoken into the fabric, into my skin. "I never wanted to hurt you like this."

I stood rigid for a moment. My body was a fence — anger on one side, exhaustion on the other — and Maya's arms were trying to pull it down. My mind was screaming caution. My heart was whispering something else. She was scared. We all were. People said things they meant when they were terrified. Maybe this was real. Maybe, beneath the layers of betrayal and performance, there was still something in Maya that remembered what we used to be. Before Phoenix. Before everything went wrong.

Her arms tightened around me, pulling me closer, and I let my guard drop. My body softened against hers. My chin rested on her shoulder, and I closed my eyes, and for one moment — one brief, fragile moment — I let myself believe that someone who had hurt me was sorry for it.

"It's okay," I whispered. The words felt uncertain on my tongue, half-believed at best. "We'll figure it out."

Her grip shifted.

It was subtle at first. The arms that had been cradling me

repositioned, hands sliding from my back to my arms, fingers wrapping around my biceps. What had been soft and enveloping became firm. Directional. Her weight shifted forward, and her feet began to move, one small step, then another, each one guiding me backward, away from the center of the room, toward the door. One hand slipped from my back; behind me, almost soundless, the bolt eased open.

My body registered the change before my mind did. The pressure of her hands and the angle of her body triggered an alarm older than language. A wrongness. A mismatch between what she was saying and what she was doing.

"Maya — " I tried to pull away, my hands pressing against her shoulders, my feet trying to plant.

Her fingers dug into my arms. Deep. Hard enough to bruise. Her face was still buried against my shoulder, but the trembling had stopped. The tears had stopped. Everything about her had become mechanical, efficient, purposeful, stripped of the emotion that had been there seconds before.

In one violent motion, she shoved.

My balance broke. My feet slid on the dusty floor, scrambling for traction, finding none. I lurched backward, arms pinwheeling, and my spine connected with the door, the handle driving into the small of my back with a bolt of pain that shot up my spine and made me gasp. The door swung open behind me — already loosened by Maya's hand — and I fell through it, my body tipping backward over the threshold.

My knees hit the hallway floor first. The impact was hard, bone against wood, a crack of pain that raced up my thighs and into my hips. My palms slapped down a second later, the shock of the cold floor stinging through my hands. I was on all fours in the dark hallway, dazed, winded, the air knocked from my lungs in a single, grunting exhale.

The door slammed shut behind me.

The sound was enormous in the empty hallway, a concussion of wood against frame that rattled the walls and sent dust sifting down from the ceiling. My ears rang. For two seconds, I was too stunned to move, too disoriented to process what had just happened. My brain was still in the room, still wrapped in Maya's arms, still believing the apology.

Then I heard the lock.

A metallic *click*. Small. Precise. Final. The sound of a bolt sliding home, of a door becoming a wall, of the last exit sealing itself shut.

I blinked. The hallway was dim, the fluorescents overhead flickering in their death-rattle rhythm, casting everything in a sickly, pulsing light. The air was cold. The floor was cold. My knees throbbed. My back ached where the door handle had struck.

"Maya?" My voice was weak, fractured, the voice of someone who already knew the answer but couldn't stop asking the question. I pushed myself up, staggering, and pressed my palms against the door. The wood was solid, unyielding, and through it I could hear nothing from the room beyond.

"Maya!" I slammed my fists against the door. The impacts were dull and flat, swallowed by the thickness of the wood. "Let me back in!"

From the other side — muffled, separated by three inches of old oak — her voice came through. Soft. Almost tender. The same tone she'd used when her arms were around me, when her tears were on my shoulder, when she was steering me toward the door.

"I'm sorry, Rose. I really am."

Six words. Delivered with the same careful precision she'd used to destroy my marriage. The same gentle, apologetic inflection that she'd probably used when she told Phoenix she loved him while I was at home, pregnant, painting a nursery seafoam green.

She'd used me. She'd played on my exhaustion, my terror, my desperate, starving need to be comforted by someone — anyone — after hours of being hunted and mocked and disbelieved. She'd wrapped her arms around me, and she'd cried on my shoulder, and every second of it had been a feint. A maneuver. A distraction to get me close enough to the door to shove me through it.

I was outside. She was inside.

I was bait.

The hallway stretched in both directions, a narrow corridor lit by fluorescent tubes that buzzed and flickered overhead, their light stuttering between dim and dimmer. The wallpaper was peeling. The floor was bare wood, warped and stained. Doors lined both sides, all closed, all dark, all silent.

And from somewhere ahead, the sound of wings.

Ahead, down the hallway, from the direction of the foyer, growing louder with each beat. The rhythm was different now. Slower. More deliberate. Each flap was a statement, his wings beat with awful patience, the cadence of something that wasn't chasing but *arriving*.

My lungs couldn't find a rhythm. The air came in short, ragged pulls that scraped my throat and never quite reached the bottom of my chest. I turned, my eyes straining against the flickering light, scanning the hallway, searching for whatever was making that sound.

He came from the shadows at the far end of the corridor.

But he wasn't on the floor.

The Creeper moved across the ceiling with a fluidity that turned his size into something weaponized and wrong, deliberate, his body inverted, his claws sunk deep into the old plaster. He crawled headfirst, his limbs splayed wide, each hand and foot finding its grip without hesitation, without sound. The claws dug in with a soft *tch-tch-tch*, a rhythmic scratching that matched the cadence of his movement, the sound of bone on wood, intimate and obscene.

His grayish-green skin stretched taut over the dark veins that webbed across his body, every one of them visible, pulsing with something that moved beneath the surface. His wings were folded tight against his back, the leathery membranes brushing the walls on either side, leaving faint marks in the dust. The shadows they cast were wrong. Too long, too dark, and they moved independently of him, slithering along the floor toward me like things with their own intent.

Those eyes found me.

Black. Bottomless. Two points of reflected light in a face that was all angles and hunger. He didn't blink. He held my gaze with the unbroken focus of something that had evolved past the need for blinking, past the need for anything that might break the connection between predator and prey. His mouth was closed, the lips pressed together, and the stillness of it — the restraint — was worse than if he'd been snarling.

He sniffed the air.

His nostrils flared wide, drawing my scent in deep enough that I could hear it from where I stood. His body stilled on the ceiling, claws embedded, every muscle locked. The sniffing wasn't casual. It was specific. Targeted. He was pulling my scent apart, separating it into its components, cataloging each one.

The gaze dropped from my face to my chest.

The damp stains had spread since the last time I'd checked, dark circles that had bled outward through the fabric of my shirt, visible even in the flickering light. My bra was saturated. The nursing pads were gone — tossed in the field hours ago — and without them, there was nothing between the milk and the world. The evidence of my body's betrayal was on full display, and the creature on the ceiling was studying it with the focused, reverent attention of something encountering the sacred.

He sniffed again. Deeper this time. The pull of it moved the air around me, as if he were drawing the hallway into his lungs one thread at a time. His eyes lit from within, black deepening around a gold center.

I tried to step back. My leg muscles clenched, the command firing from my brain —*move, step, retreat, go*— but the signal died somewhere between intention and execution. My legs were stone. My feet were rooted to the warped floorboards, and I couldn't make them lift. My body had decided, without consulting me, that running was no longer an option.

His body unfurled on the ceiling, muscles coiling, wings spreading just enough to clear the walls. His mouth opened. Not wide, just a fraction, the lips parting to reveal the edges of teeth that caught the stuttering light. The motion was deliberate. A preview. A promise.

Then he dropped.

The movement was liquid, a twisting, inverting lunge that

converted his ceiling-crawl into a downward strike without pause, without transition. One second he was above me, claws embedded in plaster. The next he was coming down, fast, silent, wings snapping open mid-descent to control the angle, claws outstretched, every line of his body aimed at me.

The last thing I saw before his shadow swallowed the light was his eyes. Gold-black. Burning. Fixed on mine with an intensity that went beyond hunger, beyond predation, into a hunger that had stopped looking only for meat.

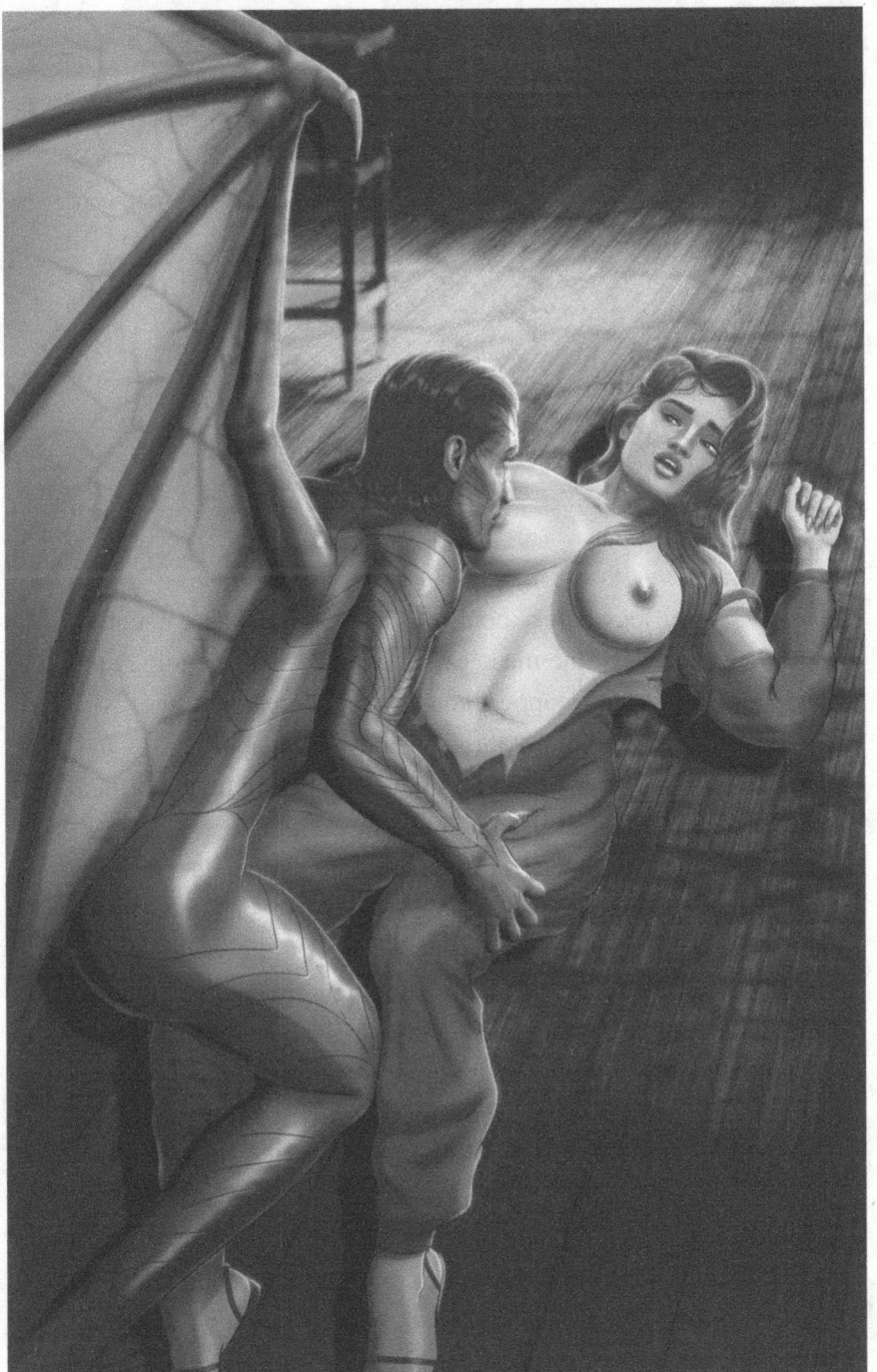

Chapter Twelve

I ran.

My legs barely held me. Each stride was a negotiation between the muscles that wanted to keep going and the joints that had stopped cooperating two hours ago. My breath burned through my throat — raw, sandpaper-dry — and the hallway stretched ahead of me in a flickering tunnel of bad light and peeling walls. Behind me, I heard him.

It wasn't the thunder of pursuit, the desperate crashing speed of something giving chase. It was worse than that. It was the slow, deliberate scraping of claws against the walls — one hand, then the other — dragging along the plaster with a measured rhythm that said everything about the distance between us and nothing about urgency. He wasn't hurrying. He didn't need to hurry. His movements carried the patience of something that had done this before, that had chased prey down corridors older than this one, and knew exactly how it would end.

I skidded into the living room, my one bare foot catching on the dusty floor. The fire had burned down to embers, casting a dim orange glow that reached the nearest furniture and stopped. The rest of the room lived in shadow. I pressed myself into the corner farthest from the door, wedging my body between the wall and a heavy armoire, and I tried to become small. Tried to fold myself into the dark and disappear.

My eyes squeezed shut. My knees pulled up to my chest. My arms wrapped around them, hugging tight, as if compressing my body could compress my scent, my warmth, my existence, shrink me down to something too small to find.

But I knew it wouldn't work. He could smell me. Alex had said he fed on fear, and if that was true, I was a banquet. Every pore on my body was broadcasting terror. In the sweat soaking through my clothes, in the milk still leaking through my shirt, in the ragged, too-fast breathing I couldn't slow down no matter how hard I tried.

The footsteps grew louder. Heavier. Each one landing massive and unhurried, the floorboards groaning under the impact. He was close. I could feel it in the way the air changed, thickening, warming, as though his body displaced the atmosphere itself. The room shrank around me.

I cracked my eyes open. Just a sliver. Just enough.

He was kneeling.

Right in front of me. Close enough that I could see the grain of his skin, grayish-green, threaded with dark veins that pulsed in slow, visible beats. His wings were folded behind him, the tips brushing the floor. His massive frame blocked the ember-light, casting me in his shadow, and those eyes — glowing gold, molten, ancient — were fixed on me with something that wasn't rage.

Curiosity.

He was studying me like something he'd never encountered before. His head tilted to one side, a birdlike motion, and his nostrils flared as he took in a deep breath. He was cataloging me. Taking inventory. And whatever he was finding, it held his attention in a way that kept his claws at his sides and his mouth closed.

I trembled. My body was a single, sustained vibration, not shaking, *vibrating,* every cell humming at the same terrified frequency. If he could smell fear, I was drenched in it. Soaked. Drowning.

He inched closer. His gaze never broke from mine. Then, with a slowness that was its own threat, he opened his mouth. His tongue slid out — forked, dark, glistening — reaching toward my face with a deliberation that turned extension into obscenity.

I braced. Every muscle locked. My teeth clenched until the hinge of my jaw ached.

The tongue touched my skin. Cold. Wet. The texture was rough, close to sandpaper, a granular surface that caught on my skin as it dragged from my jaw to my cheekbone. A slow, savoring stroke that left a trail of moisture that cooled in the air. He wasn't attacking. He was tasting. Learning me through his tongue the way a blind man reads with his fingers.

He pulled back.

The air shifted as he moved, a withdrawal, subtle but real. He was giving me space. Not out of mercy, out of something else. He sat back on his haunches, those gold eyes holding mine, and he waited. Watching me. Testing me. Seeing what I would do with the space he'd created.

Panic fired through my body, the kind of panic that demands action, anything to break the paralysis. My hand fumbled at my side, groping blindly, desperate for something, a weapon, a shield, a miracle. My fingers found fabric. Soft leather. The slipper on my right foot.

I yanked it off and threw it at him.

The motion was pure reflex, the desperate, unthinking act of a body that had run out of rational options and defaulted to the most basic one: throw something. The slipper left my hand and I watched it arc through the dim air, and in the fraction of a second between release and impact, the absurdity of what I'd just done hit me like a wall.

This wasn't a stray dog in a parking lot. This wasn't something that would flinch at a thrown shoe and slink away. He was a creature, ancient enough to make the room feel young, capable of tearing a woman apart with his bare hands. I'd just thrown a slipper at him. A *slipper*.

It hit his shoulder with a dull, soft *thud*. The sound was almost comical, a nothing-sound, the acoustic equivalent of a shrug. The slipper bounced off him and landed on the floor beside his knee.

For a moment, he went still.

Completely still. The kind of stillness that erases breathing, movement, even the pulse of those dark veins. He looked down at the slipper. Then back at me. Then down at the slipper again. His eyes narrowed, not with anger or the predatory intensity I'd seen before. With an unreadable curiosity.

He reached down and picked it up.

The slipper looked absurd in his grip, soft leather pinched between claws that could tear through bone. He lifted it to his face with a care that was startling in its gentleness. Brought it to his nose. And inhaled.

Deep. Slow. His eyes closed. His nose pressed into the fabric, brushing against it, and the breath he drew was long and savoring. The inhalation of someone encountering a scent they wanted to memorize. There was no aggression in the motion. No hunger. Just this unsettling, almost tender fascination with the object I'd thrown at him. As though it wasn't a weapon but a gift. As if the act of throwing it had been, in his understanding, something intimate.

My throat tightened. I couldn't look away. The disconnect between what I'd intended — a desperate, futile attack — and what he'd received — an offering, something to be savored — was so vast that my brain couldn't bridge it. He hadn't flinched. He hadn't retaliated. He'd *smelled my shoe.*

He tossed the slipper aside. It landed on the floor with a whisper of leather on wood, already forgotten. His focus snapped back to me, sharp, instantaneous, the switch from curiosity to something darker happening between one heartbeat and the next.

His gaze dropped to my chest.

The damp stains on my shirt had spread further, two dark, irregular circles that had bled through the fabric and were still growing, fed by the pressure and the hours without pumping. In the dim ember-light, they were impossible to miss. He leaned forward, his head lowering, his nose closing the distance between his face and the wet fabric. I pressed myself harder against the wall, my shoulders grinding into the plaster, willing it to open up and take me.

A slow, deliberate motion, tongue dragging across cracked lips, wetting them. Controlled. Anticipatory. The motion of something that had identified what it wanted and was savoring the moment before taking it.

Without warning, he tore my shirt open.

The fabric ripped with a sound that was louder than it

should have been, a tearing, parting noise that echoed off the walls and left me gasping. Cold air hit the exposed skin of my chest, and my arms crossed instinctively, trying to cover what was now bare. But he was faster. His hand — the claws retracted, the fingers blunt and surprisingly warm — brushed against my breast, and the touch made me flinch as if I'd been burned.

I felt the touch before I understood it, fingers moving across my skin, gathering the milk that had leaked and pooled along the curve. The motion was careful. Precise. Fingertips tracing the dampness with a specificity that said he knew exactly what he was collecting and exactly what it was worth.

He brought his fingers to his mouth.

The moment the milk touched his tongue, his eyes shut hard. His chest expanded with a shudder. The sound that came from him was low and broken, pulled from a place below speech. He did not feed like an animal. He fed like something that had been starving for a language and had found one in my body.

The eyes stayed closed. Lips moving, tongue working against the inside of his mouth, drawing every last trace from his fingers. The breathing had changed. Slower, deeper, the rhythm of someone lost in a moment they didn't want to end.

That was my chance.

I brought my foot up and kicked him. Hard. The ball of my foot connected with his gut, and I felt the impact travel up through my leg, solid, satisfying, the contact of flesh against something that actually gave. He rocked back, his eyes snapping open, his mouth parting in surprise. For one second — one brilliant, impossible second — I had space.

I scrambled. Hands and knees first, then feet, my body

lurching upward, every muscle firing. My bare feet slapped the floor as I pushed off, aiming for the door, for the hallway, for anywhere that wasn't here.

My right foot came down on something sharp.

The pain was instantaneous and absolute, a white-hot lance that shot from the sole of my foot up through my ankle, my calf, my thigh, all the way to my hip. I looked down and saw the shard, a piece of the wine glass Maya had dropped, thin and wicked and buried deep in the ball of my foot. Blood welled around the edges, dark and fast.

The scream left me before I could stop it. A raw, tearing sound that ripped through the room and gave away every advantage my kick had bought me.

He was on me in an instant.

His arms closed around me, an iron grip, absolute, a restraint that didn't negotiate. My body was pressed against his chest, his wings spreading wide behind him, and then the floor disappeared. The sensation of liftoff was stomach-dropping, a sudden upward lurch that pressed my organs down and stole the air from my lungs. The wind whipped past, cold and cutting, and the room spun below me as we rose.

He carried me through the mansion. The hallways blurred, dark mouths of open doors, the flicker of fluorescent light, the rush of air against my bare skin. I hung in his arms, my body limp, my foot throbbing with each pulse. The pain took up all the room I had left. I couldn't fight. Couldn't think. Could only endure.

We crashed into a room.

The impact was controlled but jarring, his feet hitting the floor with a resonant *boom* that shook the walls and rattled the old chandelier overhead. He set me down on the cold stone floor, and the chill of it seeped through my clothes immediately, pressing against my back, my shoulders, my bare legs. The room was vast, high ceilings, tall windows draped in moth-eaten curtains, a ballroom from another century, empty and echoing and cold.

I shivered. The stone was drawing the warmth out of me, and my foot screamed with every heartbeat. The shard still embedded, the blood pooling beneath it in a dark, spreading circle.

He knelt beside me.

I watched — too exhausted to do more than stare — as he reached for my foot. His movements were different now. The predatory speed was gone. In its place was something careful in a way that made it worse. His claws extended just enough to grip the shard, and he drew it out with a single, smooth pull. The glass slid free, and a fresh surge of blood followed, warm against my skin.

I hissed through my teeth, my hands fisting at my sides.

He set the shard aside. Then he reached up and tore a strip of fabric from the nearest curtain. A strip he wound around my foot with a precision that didn't belong to a creature who had just been hunting me through a mansion. Each wrap was tight but not too tight, the pressure even, the knot secured against the arch of my foot with a deftness that made my throat close.

Why?

The question hammered at the inside of my skull. Why help me? Why remove the glass, bandage the wound, handle me with care that bordered on tenderness? Five minutes ago, he'd been chasing me. An hour ago, he'd torn Sophie apart. The contrast was so violent that my brain couldn't hold both truths at the same time. It kept switching between them, trying to reconcile the creature who killed with the one who was kneeling at my feet, wrapping my wound with torn curtain.

But before I could find an answer — before I could even form the next question — the change happened.

His eyes.

They shifted. The clinical focus he'd applied to my wound dissolved, and what replaced it was something older, darker, more fundamental. His gaze moved from my foot to my chest, where the torn fabric of my shirt hung open, where the skin was still damp, where the dark circles of leaked milk were visible against my skin. His breathing changed. Quickened, deepened, each inhale pulling more air, each exhale releasing it in a slow drag I could feel against my body.

The hunger was back. But it was different now. Braided with recognition until I couldn't tell where one ended and the other began. He wanted permission. He already knew the answer.

He moved closer.

The fabric tore before I realized he'd gripped it. The remaining shirt parted with a soft rip, and the cold air hit my bare chest. My arms came up, instinct, modesty, the desperate muscle-memory of a woman who had spent a year hating her own body. He caught my wrists and held them, not roughly, but firmly. The grip of something that wanted access and was willing to wait exactly long enough for resistance to end.

His head lowered. I felt his breath first, brushing against the skin of my breast. Then his mouth.

The contact was a jolt. Lips closing around my nipple, the heat of his mouth sudden and electric and wrong in ways I didn't have language for. Teeth grazed the sensitive skin — light, testing — and then came the suck. Deep, deliberate, greedy in its rhythm, and I could feel the milk responding, letting down in a warm rush that met his hunger and fed it.

My body jolted at the contact. A gasp tore from my throat — involuntary, sharp — and my hands clenched into fists, nails biting into my palms. His grip on my wrists held me in place while his mouth worked, pulling at me with a force that sent sensation radiating outward from the point of contact. Through my chest, down my spine, pooling in places I didn't want to acknowledge.

His other hand moved. The claws retracted. I felt it happen, the subtle shift of bone and keratin withdrawing into his fingers, and what touched me next was skin. Warm, rough-textured skin, the pads of his fingers pressing against my thigh, sliding upward with a precision that was too knowing, too specific to be accidental.

I squeezed my thighs together. The reflex was instant, desperate, my muscles clamping down, trying to create a barrier, trying to stop what was happening. He paused. His hand rested on my leg, motionless, the pressure steady and patient. Then, with a strength that made the effort feel trivial, he parted them.

Fingers found the edge of my underwear. Pushed past it. And when they brushed against me — against the most sensitive, most private part of my body — the sound that left my mouth was not a scream.

It was a whimper.

A broken sound left him. Because my body was responding. The touch, which should have produced nothing but revulsion, nothing but the cold, shutting-down reflex of violation, was producing heat. Warmth spreading outward from where his fingers moved, slow and specific, finding the places that made my breath hitch and returning to them. My mind screamed at my body to stop, to refuse, to go numb. My body didn't listen.

He switched to my other breast. His mouth latched on with renewed hunger, each suck deeper, more insistent, pulling at me with a force that sent jolts straight to my core. I gasped. My hips lifted. An involuntary, shameful motion that I couldn't prevent and couldn't take back. His fingers moved lower, sliding inside me with an ease that made my face burn, his thumb maintaining pressure on the spot that was turning my thoughts to static.

I didn't want this. I didn't want any of this. The words repeated in my head. A mantra, a prayer, a desperate attempt to maintain the boundary between what I was experiencing and what I was choosing. My mind said no. My body answered anyway. Every nerve was alight. Every sensation was amplified. His mouth on my breast, his fingers inside me, the dual rhythm of sucking and stroking. It built pressure inside me that I couldn't stop, couldn't slow, couldn't redirect.

The orgasm crashed through me without permission.

It hit like a seizure, my back arching off the stone floor, my muscles locking, my vision whiting out at the edges. The sound I made was wrenched from me. Not a moan, not a cry, but the space between them, dragged from a place deeper than my throat, a place I didn't know existed until this moment. My legs trembled, my hands clawed at the stone beneath me, and the waves kept coming, each one pulling tighter before releasing, over and over, until my body had wrung itself empty.

The sob came after.

It broke through the aftermath, something held underwater and finally surfaced. Tears streamed down my temples, running into my hair, soaking the stone beneath my head. I hated this. I hated him. I hated my body for its treason. For feeling pleasure where there should have been only violation, for responding to a monster's touch as though it were a thing wanted, a gift chosen.

His mouth released me with a wet sound. When I forced myself to look at him, his face was wet with my milk — glistening across his lips and chin — and his eyes held a satisfaction that went beyond physical satiation. He looked anchored, a creature that had drifted for centuries and finally touched bottom.

The withdrawal was slow. Fingers sliding out of me as though memorizing the path. Every small aftershock that ran through my body seemed to feed something in him. He watched each tremor, each involuntary clench, with the attentive focus of someone observing something they'd caused and were proud of.

Then, to my shock, he settled beside me.

His body lowered to the floor, massive, heavy, his wings folding behind him. He curled against my side, his head dipping toward my chest, his breathing slowing into something that almost resembled rest. His claws extended again, slowly, the keratin sliding out from his fingertips with a soft, clicking sound, and the gesture read like a seal. He'd finished what he came for. The predator had fed, and now the predator was at ease.

The ballroom was quiet. His breathing, my breathing, and the distant drip of rain through a cracked window, that was all.

Chapter Thirteen

I lay still. My mind was a wreck, images and sensations tumbling over each other, none of them making sense. His tenderness with the glass shard. His hunger at my breast. The orgasm I hadn't wanted and couldn't deny. The creature curled against me like something tame, something satisfied, something that had mistaken what just happened for intimacy.

My fingers moved without my telling them to. They crept across the cold stone floor, searching, feeling the texture of dust and grit beneath my fingertips until they brushed against cold metal.

An old candelabra. Heavy, iron, three-armed, lying on its side against the base of a column.

My pulse kicked.

The eyes were closed. Breathing deepened. The body beside me was heavy and warm, wings lying flat, membranes relaxed. He wasn't watching me. He wasn't listening. Whatever guard he maintained during the hunt had been lowered in the aftermath, and he lay beside me with the unguarded trust of something that had never been hurt by the thing it rested against.

My fingers wrapped around the candelabra's stem. The iron was cold enough to sting, and the candelabra settled into my grip, solid and cold, a rightness that made my breath come faster. This was a weapon. The first real weapon I'd had since the nightmare began.

I swung.

Every ounce of strength I had left went into the motion, arms extending, shoulders rotating, core engaging, the candelabra cutting through the air in a tight, vicious arc that ended against the side of his skull.

The impact was a sound I'd never heard before and never wanted to hear again. Wet. Solid. The *thock* of dense metal meeting bone through a layer of skin and muscle, followed by a deeper, cracking sound beneath, the sound of structure giving way. The candelabra bit into his temple and stuck, the metal embedding itself in the fracture it had created.

Blood sprayed. Hot, dark, immediate, a fan of droplets that hit the floor and my arm and the stone column behind him. He jerked away from me, his body rolling, his eyes snapping open. They were wide with shock, as if the possibility of being struck had never occurred to him. His mouth opened, and the sound that came out was wet and rattling, more startled than hurt.

I didn't wait.

I swung again. The candelabra came around in a shorter, tighter arc, no windup this time, just raw, desperate force. It connected with his skull a second time, and the crunch was different, louder, wetter, the sound of bone that had already been weakened giving way entirely. His head wrenched to the side, and blood poured — not sprayed, *poured*— from the wound, running down his face and his neck, pooling in the hollow of his collarbone.

He snarled. The sound was low, controlled, vibrating through the floor and up into my chest. But he didn't strike. His hand came up to his head, fingers pressing into the wound, and when he pulled them away, they were slick and dark. He gripped the candelabra — which was still embedded in his skull — and yanked it free. The sound of metal pulling through torn flesh was something my stomach couldn't handle. Bile surged, hot and sour, and I choked it back.

The wound gaped. Through the blood and the torn skin, I could see bone, pale, cracked, the surface glistening with something wet and organic. Beneath the bone, a darker layer, raw, pulsing tissue that moved with each beat of whatever passed for his heart.

Then it began to close.

I watched it happen. Watched the bone knit, edges reaching toward each other, fusing, the fracture sealing itself, a crack filled with mortar. Skin followed, stretching over the newly repaired bone, pulling taut, smoothing, until the wound was gone. Gone, fresh skin, unmarked, as if the candelabra had never touched him. As if the last thirty seconds had been erased from his body.

He looked at me. Blood still coated the left side of his face, but beneath it, nothing. Whole. Unmarked. As if I had never touched him. The same face that had studied me in the living room, that had pressed against my breast, that had kneeled at my feet and bandaged my wound. Unbroken.

Whatever restraint I had left broke.

I got to my feet. The pain in my foot was a distant thing,

present but irrelevant, pushed to the margins by the adrenaline flooding my system. I ran. Limping, lurching, my bare feet slapping the stone, the bandage on my right foot already soaking through with fresh blood.

He flew.

The wind from his wings hit my back — a hard, shoving gust — and then his weight was on me. He caught me from above, his body driving mine to the floor, his legs straddling my hips, his hands pinning my wrists against the cold stone. I thrashed beneath him. My arms wrenched against his grip. My legs kicked, useless, wild, connecting with nothing. I twisted, arched, bucked, anything to get him off. Nothing worked. He was too strong. His weight pressed down on me, immovable, and his claws dug into my skin just enough to remind me that struggling was a choice with consequences.

Then he screeched.

The sound split the air, a piercing, glass-scraping shriek that drove into my eardrums and ricocheted through my skull. My body went rigid beneath the assault of it, every muscle seizing. And then his face began to change.

The skin pulled back. Not gradually. It peeled, retreating from the center of his face toward the edges, drawing tight over the bones beneath. His mouth stretched. Wider than a mouth should stretch, wider than anatomy allowed, the corners splitting, the skin tearing along invisible seams, until the entire lower half of his face was a gaping, wet cavern lined with rows of teeth. Not human teeth. Rows. Layered. Each one narrow, curved, glistening with saliva that dripped from the points and ran in thin streams down his chin.

But it was the mandibles that made the world stop.

They emerged from the sides of his face, two jointed,

segmented structures, insect-like, armored in dark chitin that gleamed under the dim light. They unfolded outward in a slow, clicking extension, each segment locking into place with a wet, mechanical snap. The mandibles were lined with serrations, fine, sharp, designed for gripping and tearing. Thin strands of mucus stretched between them, catching the light, and the sound they made as they opened and closed — a rapid, rhythmic *clack-clack-clack*— was the sound of something that had stopped pretending to be anything other than what it was.

His face was no longer a face. It was a feeding apparatus. A biological machine designed for a single function, wearing human features the way a mask wears an expression. Convenience, camouflage, as the thinnest possible barrier between what you saw and what was underneath.

Those eyes locked onto mine. Gold-black. Burning. And in them, no mercy, no curiosity, no restraint. Just the fathomless hunger of something that had been alive for centuries and had never once been satisfied.

I opened my mouth to scream. No sound came out. My throat had closed, my lungs had locked, and the terror was so total, so complete, that it had shut down the systems required to express it. I was silent. Immobile. Pinned beneath something that was about to kill me, and I couldn't even scream.

I knew I was going to die.

And then, a noise.

Distant. Soft. The groan of hinges. A door, somewhere in the house, creaking open.

His head snapped up. The mandibles froze mid-click, hovering open. His nostrils flared, pulling in air from the direction of the sound. His posture changed, the predatory focus that had been aimed entirely at me shifted, redirected, pointed at whatever had just entered his territory.

He hissed — a low, rushing sound that I felt against my face — and then, with a final snarl that vibrated through my bones, he launched himself off me. His wings opened with a violent snap, and the downdraft hit me like a shove, rolling me across the stone floor. I curled onto my side, gasping, as the sound of his wings receded down the hallway. Fast, furious, aimed at something I couldn't see.

I lay on the cold stone. Gasping. Shaking. Every inch of my body was trembling, a fine, deep vibration running through muscle and bone, the shaking of a system pushed past its tolerances that hadn't yet decided whether to recover or shut down.

I reached for the nearest curtain — a heavy, moth-eaten drape that hung from a broken rod — and pulled it down. The fabric was dusty and stiff, but I wrapped it around my body, covering the torn shirt, the bare skin, the evidence of everything that had just happened. It didn't make me feel safe. Nothing was going to make me feel safe. But it was a barrier, however thin, between my body and the air, and in that moment, a barrier was all I had.

The sounds started.

From the hallway. From somewhere below. Screams, raw, male, ragged with terror. And beneath the screams, the other sounds. The wet ones. The tearing ones. The sounds of a body being separated from itself, one piece at a time.

I didn't want to know. Every rational part of my mind was screaming to stay where I was, to stay wrapped in the curtain, curled on the floor, invisible and silent and still. But my body had already started moving. My hands pressed against the stone. My legs pushed. And before I could stop myself, I was at the door of the ballroom, peering around the frame into the dim hallway beyond.

Brian was in the Creeper's grip.

Those massive claws were wrapped around Brian's throat, lifting him off the ground as if he were made of paper. Brian's feet kicked, frantic, useless arcs that connected with nothing. His face was flushed dark red, the veins in his temples standing out like cords, his eyes bulging with the pressure of restricted blood flow. His hands clawed at the creature's wrist, nails scraping skin that didn't mark.

Alex stood just within reach. Rigid. Trembling. His eyes were locked on the scene before him, and I could read the battle on his face, the war between wanting to help and wanting to survive, each impulse canceling the other, leaving him paralyzed in the space between.

From somewhere below — the living room, the foyer, I couldn't tell — Katie screamed. One short, sharp sound that cut off too fast, followed by a heavy impact. A body hitting the floor.

Moments later I heard Brian's voice, "Help me!" He choked. The words were wet, strangled, forced through a throat that was being compressed. His arm flailed toward Alex, fingers grasping at the air. "Help me, man!"

Alex's foot shifted. One small step. Then it stopped.

Brian's face contorted. And what I saw there was calculation, not desperation. In the space between one ragged breath and the next, Brian made his choice. His hand shot out, hooked into Alex's shirt, and dragged him forward. Alex stumbled, pulled off-balance by Brian's weight and thrown straight into the Creeper's line of sight. His arms pinwheeled. His face registered the betrayal a full second before his body under-stood what had happened.

"Take him!" Brian's scream was shrill, cracking. "Not me! Take HIM!"

The Creeper's eyes shifted to Alex. A pause, brief, clinical, the assessment of a predator evaluating new prey. Then his free hand moved. The claws caught the light for one frozen instant before they slashed through the air and into Alex's chest.

The sound was wet fabric tearing. Alex's body jerked — a single, violent spasm — and his mouth opened in a silent, airless gasp. Blood bloomed across his shirt, spreading fast, and his hands came up to the wound, pressing against it in a futile attempt to hold himself together.

I couldn't stay hidden. My body moved, launching forward, out of the ballroom doorway, across the hallway. I threw myself between them, between Alex and the Creeper, my arms spread wide, my body a barrier that I knew was insuf-ficient but offered anyway.

"Stop!"

The Creeper paused. His claws hovered. Inches from my face, close enough that I could see the blood on them, could smell the iron, could feel the displaced air from the aborted strike. His eyes found mine, and what I saw there was some-thing that might have been curiosity, or recognition, or the faintest flicker of the thing that had made him bandage my foot.

But it wasn't enough.

Behind me, Alex was falling. I heard it, the wet, staggering sound of a man whose body was failing him, whose legs were buckling under the weight of blood loss and shock. His breath came in ragged, drowning gasps. His hands slipped from his chest, leaving dark, glistening prints on his shirt.

The Creeper's claws moved.

The strike was fast, faster than the first. He shifted one inch, enough to make me useless as a shield. The strike went past me, over my shoulder, with a precision that spoke of something that had been killing for centuries and could thread a needle with its claws. They tore through Alex's torso — flesh, muscle, bone — with a sound I would carry for the rest of my life. A wet, ripping sound, followed by a choked, gurgling cry that cut off midway, replaced by the soft, terrible sound of a body hitting the floor.

Alex was still.

The Creeper stood over him, his chest moving with slow control. His eyes dropped to the body at his feet, watching the last movement — a twitch, a final tremor — fade to nothing. Blood spread in a dark pool that crept across the floorboards, reaching the edge of my bare foot.

I wanted to scream. The scream was right there, in my throat, in my chest, pressing against the inside of my ribs like something trying to break free. But it wouldn't come. The horror was too complete, too absolute, and it had locked everything down. My voice, my legs, my ability to process what I was seeing.

Brian saw his chance. With the Creeper's attention on Alex's body, Brian tried to back away, slow, careful, his breath coming in ragged, shaking gasps, his eyes fixed on the creature. His feet shuffled backward, one inch at a time.

The Creeper's head turned.

Slowly. The motion was unhurried, almost lazy, the rotation of a predator that knows its prey has nowhere to go. His eyes locked onto Brian, and the smile that spread across his face was the most terrible thing I had seen all night, worse than the mandibles, worse than the regeneration, worse than any of it. Because the smile was *pleased*. He was enjoying this.

He moved toward Brian like a cat toward a cornered mouse, slow, deliberate, each step a performance, each pause an opportunity for the prey to fully appreciate what was coming. His claws flexed, extending and retracting, the tips catching the light in dull flashes.

Brian broke.

"Please — " His voice was thin, shredded. "Please, no. Please!"

The Creeper didn't listen. He never listened. He grabbed Brian by the throat again — lifting him, one-handed, his arm extended, Brian's feet dangling — and the other hand rose. The claws traced a line down Brian's chest, slow, almost tender, the tip of each claw dimpling the skin without breaking it. A preview. A promise of what was coming.

Then the claws pressed in.

I turned. I couldn't watch. My body spun on instinct, and I staggered away from the hallway, my hands pressed against my ears, trying to block the sounds. But hands weren't enough. Nothing was enough. Brian's screams, raw, piercing, screams that change something fundamental in the person who hears them, pushed through my palms and into my skull, filling every space, every silence.

The sounds went on. And on. The Creeper was taking his time. The flesh separated from bone in steady pulls, methodical, paced, savored. Brian's screams changed. From words to sounds to wet, choking gurgles that were worse than the screams because they meant the capacity for screaming had been damaged.

And then they stopped.

I climbed the stairs. One at a time. Each step was a negotiation with my body, the injured foot screaming, the uninjured foot trembling, my hands gripping the banister with white-knuckled desperation. The shadows on the stairwell walls twisted and stretched, reaching for me, and Brian's screams were still echoing in my skull, layered over the image of Alex, broken, still, the blood spreading.

I reached the upstairs hallway. I stumbled to the nearest door. Pushed it open. The room was dark, cold, dominated by a heavy wooden bed frame with a dusty mattress. I didn't turn on the light. I didn't look around. I dropped to my knees, lowered myself to the floor, and crawled beneath the bed.

The darkness closed around me. The smell of mildew filled my lungs. The underside of the mattress hung low enough to brush my back, and the floor beneath me was cold and gritty with dust that hadn't been disturbed in years.

I curled onto my side. My knees drew up. My arms wrapped around them.

And in the dark, in the silence that wasn't really silence, because the Creeper was still out there, still moving through the house, still wet with the blood of the people I'd come here with. I closed my eyes and waited for whatever was coming next.

Chapter Fourteen

I stayed curled beneath the bed until my body forgot I was afraid and remembered it was exhausted.

The two sensations had been fighting each other for hours — fear pulling me taut, fatigue dragging me down — and at some point the fatigue won. More like a machine shutting down when you pull its plug, not the clean surrender of falling asleep in your own bed: one system after another going dark, the processes stopping mid-cycle, the body committing to rest because the alternative, staying conscious in this house, in this dark, with the sounds from the hallway still reverberating through the floorboards, was no longer sustainable.

The mildew smell was thick enough to chew. The underside of the mattress sagged low, close enough to brush my shoulder when I shifted. The floor beneath me was cold, gritty, coated in a layer of dust that had settled over years and compressed into something almost like felt. My injured foot throbbed in time with my heartbeat, a dull, metronomic ache that eventually blended into the background noise of my body and stopped demanding attention.

I closed my eyes. And the dark behind my eyelids was no different from the dark in front of them, and at some point the distinction stopped mattering, and I was gone.

Time dissolved.

I had no idea how long I slept. Minutes. Hours. The concept of duration had lost its meaning in this house, where every room looked the same, where the windows were boarded, where the only clocks were biological, heartbeat, breath, the slow accumulation of hunger and thirst and the pressure building in my chest again, the milk with nowhere to go.

What woke me wasn't a sound.

It was a presence.

The air beside me had changed, thickened, warmed. A body displaced the space next to mine. Alive, breathing, radiating heat in the uneven pattern of a person who was trying very hard not to be noticed.

My body went rigid before my brain caught up. Every muscle locked, arms, legs, jaw, the muscles along my spine pulling taut, guy wires on a mast. My breath caught in my throat and stayed there, trapped between the exhale I'd been making and the inhale I couldn't start.

Someone was under the bed with me.

I turned my head. Slowly. The motion was glacial, a centimeter at a time, my neck rotating with the controlled care of someone disarming a bomb, my eyes straining in the dark to resolve whatever shape was lying inches away.

Maya.

Her face was close enough that I could feel her breath on my cheek, rapid, shallow, each exhale carrying the chemical sharpness of cocaine and fear-sweat. Her skin was pale beneath the streaks of blood that ran from a cut above her hairline down across her left eye and cheek, the blood partially dried, cracking along the lines of her expression. Her clothes hung from her body in strips. Torn, shredded, the fabric blackened with stains I didn't examine closely. Her hair was matted, tangled with plaster dust and something darker.

She was shaking. Not trembling, shaking. A full-body convulsion that ran through her in continuous waves, each one strong enough that I could feel it through the floorboards beneath us, a vibration carried through the wood from her body to mine.

Her eyes found me. Wide. Wet. The pupils blown so large that the irises had nearly disappeared, leaving two dark circles in a white field. When she spoke, her lips barely moved, the words pushed out through a jaw that was clenched too tight to open properly.

"It... it killed them." Each word was a separate effort, forced past the blockage in her throat. Her hand twitched, fingers clawing weakly at the floor between us. "Brian... Alex..." A hiccup broke through — half sob, half gasp — and her face crumpled for a second before she pulled it back into shape. "I think Katie too. I-I don't know." Her breath caught, and the next words came out fast and broken. "I saw Brian. I saw Alex. I didn't wait long enough to see Katie." She swallowed hard and looked away. "I just ran."

The words sank into me, settling in my stomach, stones dropped into water. Brian. Alex. Katie. Dead. Or dying. The people I'd come here with, the ones I'd argued with, the ones I'd tried to warn, the ones who had laughed and dismissed and mocked and, in their own flawed ways, existed in my life, were gone.

143

And Maya was here. Under my bed. Alive.

The memory hit me hard enough to turn my stomach. Maya's arms around me. The tears on my shoulder. The warmth of her body. And then the shift, the grip changing, the feet moving, the violent shove that sent me through the door, the click of the lock, and her voice through three inches of oak: *I'm sorry, Rose. I really am.*

She had fed me to the Creeper. Wrapped me in a false embrace and pushed me into the hallway like a sacrifice on a slab. She'd used my exhaustion, my terror, my desperate, starving need for comfort. Weaponized all of it, played it like an instrument, and then shut the door and listened from the other side.

And now she was here. Under the bed. Next to me. Shaking. Seeking the protection of the woman she'd offered up as bait.

Maya had always been this. Always. Even before Phoenix, before the affair, before any of it. She was the woman who survived by making sure someone else didn't. She was the lifeboat that threw people overboard to keep from sinking. She'd done it to me at the door, and she'd done it to the others. I could see it on her, in the strips of torn clothing and the blood that wasn't all hers, in the wild, animal desperation of someone who had watched people die and chosen to run.

She left them behind. Just like she left me.

Her eyes darted toward the bedroom door, visible from beneath the bed as a vertical line of dim light at the threshold. Her body pressed closer to mine, seeking warmth, seeking shelter, seeking the proximity of another living body as though physical closeness could create safety.

She didn't deserve it. She didn't deserve any of it.

Then came the wings.

The sound built from nothing, a whisper that grew, one beat at a time, each flap heavier and more deliberate than the last. The rhythm was slow. Patient. The cadence of something that wasn't searching but arriving, that knew exactly where it was going and was in no rush to get there. The beats grew louder, the vibrations pushing through the walls, through the floor, through the bedframe above us until the mattress springs hummed in sympathy.

Maya stiffened beside me. Her breathing, which had been rapid and ragged, stopped entirely, a held breath, suspended, in case exhaling might draw the creature's attention. Her eyes locked on the door. Her body went still in the way that only absolute terror can produce. Not calm. Not controlled. Paralyzed. The stillness of a rabbit that has heard the hawk and is betting everything on being invisible.

I chose.

It rose from a place I didn't know I had, a deep, subterranean chamber somewhere beneath the grief and the fear and the exhaustion, a room I'd never entered until tonight. What climbed out of it was dark. Quiet. Certain. Not rage. I'd burned through rage hours ago, spent it on Brian and Maya in the living room, left it scattered across the floor with the broken wine glass. This was something colder. More deliberate. A recognition that the universe had arranged itself into a specific configuration, and all I had to do was let it play out.

It was her turn.

The door creaked open.

He entered the room the way smoke enters a space, slowly, filling every corner, displacing the air. His grayish-green body moved with a deliberate grace that was somehow worse than speed, each step placed with precision, his bare feet silent on the wooden floor. His wings folded inward, tight against his back, the membranes brushing the doorframe as he passed through. The room — which had felt large when I'd crawled under the bed — contracted around him, the walls pulling closer, the ceiling pressing down.

His black eyes swept the space. Slow. Methodical. The bed. The dresser. The window. The closet. He was cataloging the room, reading it like a hunter reads terrain, and the inevitability of what was coming pressed down on me like a fact I already knew.

I moved.

Silently. My body slid out from under the bed on the side farthest from the door, arms first, then torso, then legs, the motion slow and controlled, each inch covered without sound. The dust beneath me shifted, and I held my breath until I was clear, until I was standing in the far corner of the room with the cold wall against my back and the Creeper between me and the bed.

He registered my presence. His eyes found me — those bottomless, glowing eyes — and interest moved in them. He wasn't surprised. He'd expected to find me here. What he hadn't expected was for me to be standing.

I looked at him. He looked at me. And between us, under the bed, Maya's breathing had become audible — fast, shallow, panicked — the sound of someone who knew she'd been found and was trying to crawl deeper into a space that had no depth.

I raised my hand. Extended one finger. And I pointed at the bed.

"She's under there."

My voice was calm. The words came out level and clear, unshaking, stripped of everything except the information they carried. Three words. A direction. A delivery.

The Creeper's head tilted. A slow, birdlike rotation, his chin dropping, his eyes narrowing. Curiosity crossed his face, or perhaps the recognition of a transaction being offered. He looked at the bed. Then back at me. Then at the bed again.

He moved forward.

"Rose!" Maya's hiss came from beneath the mattress, thin, cracking, the sound of a voice being squeezed through a throat too tight with panic. "What are you doing?" I could hear her nails scraping the floor, hear the desperate scrabbling of her body trying to push itself deeper into a corner that didn't exist. "Please, don't —"

The Creeper crouched beside the bed. His head lowered, tilting, those dark eyes peering into the gap between mattress and floor. He could see her. I could see the moment he locked on, a subtle shift in his posture, a tightening of his shoulders, the focused stillness of a predator that has located its target and no longer needs to search.

He gripped the bedframe.

One hand. His claws curled under the wooden rail, and the muscles in his arm bunched — a single, effortless contraction — and the bed came up. The entire thing — frame, mattress, box spring — ripped from its position and tossed aside with a crash that shook the walls, the headboard splintering against the far corner, the mattress folding in on itself as it hit the floor.

Maya was exposed.

She lay on the bare floor in a fetal curl, her arms wrapped around her head, her knees drawn up, her body compressed into the smallest possible shape. The shaking had intensified, violent, full-body tremors that rattled her teeth and made her joints jump. Her eyes were screwed shut, as if she could make the creature unreal by refusing to see it.

Then she opened them. And she looked at me.

"Please!" The word tore out of her, raw and desperate, her hands reaching toward me, fingers outstretched, grasping at the air between us. "Don't let him do this! Rose, please!"

I stood in the corner of the room, my back against the cold wall, and I watched her. Her face, streaked with blood, twisted with terror, wet with tears that cut clean tracks through the grime, was the face of someone who had reached the end of everything and found nothing there to save her. Her mouth moved, shaping words, shaping pleas, shaping the name she'd once used casually, over coffee, over wine, during the years when she was smiling at me and sleeping with my husband.

I said nothing.

He gripped her ankle.

Maya's scream pierced the room, high, sustained, the sound of someone whose body had exceeded its capacity for controlled response and was simply outputting raw audio. He dragged her across the floor, her back scraping the bare wood, her hands scrabbling for purchase, her nails catching on the grain and peeling backward, leaving thin red smears on the boards.

Satisfaction stirred in me as I watched. It had been growing all night, through the gaslighting, through the shove, through the locked door and the soft "I'm sorry", and now it had found its full shape.

She was feeling it. What I had felt in the hallway, when the lock clicked and the cold hit my skin and I realized I'd been fed to a monster by someone who was supposed to love me. The helplessness. The betrayal. The absolute, shattering understanding that the person you trusted had calculated your worth and decided you were expendable.

Maya was feeling all of it. And the creature was watching me while he did it.

His dark eyes flicked to mine, a glance, quick but deliberate, as though confirming something. Seeking something. Approval. Permission. The acknowledgment that what he was about to do was sanctioned by the one person in the room whose opinion he valued.

I held his gaze. I didn't nod. I didn't speak. But I didn't look away.

He grinned. The expression spread across his face, his smile spread, the rows of sharp teeth catching the dim light. It was the grin of something that had received what it needed and was ready to proceed.

Claws found her legs. The tips pressed in — deliberate, controlled — and drew downward in slow, even strokes, parting the skin in thin, precise lines that welled dark red before the blood began to flow. Maya's body convulsed, her hips bucking, her hands slapping the floor in desperate, futile resistance. The sound she made was no longer a scream. It was lower, rougher, a keening moan that spoke of pain beyond the capacity of screaming.

Blood pooled beneath her, spreading across the boards in dark, creeping tendrils. Her clothes — what remained of them — soaked through in seconds, the fabric changing color, darkening, clinging to her skin. The Creeper worked with patience. No rush. No frenzy. Each stroke of his claws was measured, spaced, the intervals between them long enough for the pain to register fully before the next one arrived.

Maya's moans became words. Broken, gasping, pushed through teeth that were clenched against the agony.

"Rose... please..." Her eyes found mine across the room. Wet. Dimming. The light behind them guttering. "I'm sorry... I didn't mean it... I didn't..."

I heard them. I understood them. And I felt nothing.

He pulled her upward. His claws sank into the flesh of her shoulders, lifting her from the floor, her body hanging, her head lolling to one side. Blood slid from her mouth, the result of something torn inside that was leaking into the wrong spaces. Her breath was shallow, her chest barely moving, the rise and fall so faint that it was visible only as a slight tremor in the blood-soaked fabric of her shirt.

The mouth found her shoulder. Teeth sank in, a tearing, a wrenching pull that separated flesh from bone with a sound that was wet and fibrous and final. Blood sprayed, a hot, arterial fan that hit the far wall and ran downward in long, branching streaks. Maya's body jerked in his grip, a spasm that was more mechanical than conscious, the reflexive firing of nerves that no longer had a functioning brain to report to.

He kept his eyes on me.

Through every second of it, the tearing, the spraying, the sounds that I would hear in my sleep for the rest of my life, his eyes stayed locked on mine. He watched me watching. He fed on her body and he fed on my reaction, and the two hungers were tangled together in a way that I understood without wanting to, without trying to, without being able to stop understanding.

He dropped her. The body, it was a body now, not a person,

the distinction made in the instant between the last breath and the first second of stillness, hit the floor with a dull, soft sound. He wasn't finished. His claws found her stomach. One motion. One brutal, downward pull that opened her from sternum to hip, the sound filling the room, wet fabric ripped apart.

Maya's eyes were open. They stared at the ceiling, fixed on something none of us could see. Her chest didn't move. Her hands lay at her sides, the fingers curled inward, the nails bloody and broken.

The room went silent.

He stood. His chest rose and fell with his breathing steadied, the respiration of something that had exerted itself and was settling. His hands were coated, dark, glistening, the blood beginning to cool and thicken on his skin. He wiped his claws across the shreds of Maya's clothing, a deliberate, unhurried motion, cleaning himself with the remains of what he'd destroyed.

Then he turned to me.

His dark eyes held a satisfaction that I recognized because I'd felt it myself, the dark, complete satisfaction of something owed and delivered, a debt settled in the only currency that had ever mattered. He looked at me as though he'd done this for me. As though Maya's death were a gift. An offering. The monster's version of flowers.

And the terrible, unspeakable truth was that I had wanted it. I had stood in the corner and watched and said nothing and felt the satisfaction move through me like warm water, and I had wanted her to suffer the way I had suffered, and I had gotten what I wanted.

The realization hit me after the fact. The way a wave hits after the undertow has already pulled you off your feet. My stomach clenched. The nausea slammed up my throat, a physical rejection of what I'd just witnessed and what I'd just been. My hand flew to my mouth. My body folded forward, my breath coming in sharp, panicked gasps that tasted like bile and copper and the stale air of a room that smelled like blood.

I backed away. One step, then another, then faster, my bare feet sliding on the blood-slicked floor. The Creeper watched me, his head tilting, those dark eyes narrowing, registering the shift in my body language, the change from stillness to retreat.

My legs moved before my mind agreed. I turned and I ran.

The hallway swallowed me. Dark, narrow, winding. The corridors of this mansion had been designed for a different century, a different purpose, and they twisted through the house like arteries, branching and reconnecting in patterns that made no sense. My bare feet slapped the cold wood, the sound echoing ahead of me and behind me simultaneously, making it impossible to tell which direction my own footsteps were coming from.

Behind me — above me — the wings. Low growls rolled through the corridor, reverberating off the walls, and the rhythmic beating of them pushed air against my back in steady, pulsing waves. He was behind me. Closing. Not rushing. The pace was controlled, deliberate, the pursuit of something that was enjoying the chase as much as it would enjoy the catch.

Claws grazed my back.

The contact was light, a brush, a skim, the tips of his claws tracing a line across my shoulder blades, but the sensation that shot through me was anything but light. Electric. A jolt ran down my spine and branched outward, making my skin prickle and my breath catch. Not pain. A pleasure next door to pain.

I stumbled. My injured foot caught on a warped floorboard

and my balance shifted, my body lurching forward, my hands reaching for a wall that was farther than I expected. I caught myself — barely — and kept moving, my stride shortened, my momentum compromised.

He caught me at the end of the corridor.

The curtain I'd wrapped around my body was torn away. A single, ripping motion that stripped the curtain from my shoulders and left it in a crumpled heap on the floor behind me. The cold air hit my bare skin, and every nerve fired at once, with exposure, with the vulnerable awareness of being uncovered in the presence of something that was looking.

And he was looking. His eyes moved over me in the dim hallway light. Slow, deliberate, taking in every curve and line and shadow with the focused attention of something that was memorizing what it saw. His gaze was heavy. Physical. I could feel it on my skin the way I felt temperature, the way I felt the air move, a tangible force that raised the fine hairs on my arms and tightened the muscles in my stomach.

He lunged.

His body hit mine and drove me backward into the wall, the impact knocking the air from my lungs in a single, compressed gasp. His hands closed around my wrists and pinned them above my head, one hand, both wrists, the grip absolute. His body pressed against mine, his weight holding me in place, and his face was inches from my face, his breath coming in warm, uneven gusts that brushed my lips.

The gold burned low and deep when those eyes searched mine, and behind the hunger and the predatory focus, there was something else, something I'd seen flashes of throughout the night. When he'd picked up the slipper and smelled it. When he'd removed the glass from my foot. When he'd watched me watching Maya die. A question. An attempt to understand something about me that didn't fit his categories.

He stared at me as if I were a language he was trying to learn. As if the things I'd done tonight, the slipper, the candelabra, giving him Maya, standing in the corner and refusing to look away. Had presented him with data he couldn't process. I had fought him and fed him. I had run from him and handed him a victim. I had hit him hard enough to crack his skull and then stood still while he killed the woman who betrayed me.

He couldn't figure me out. And the not-knowing was holding him here, pinned against me, studying my face from inches away instead of doing whatever his instincts were demanding.

I don't know what came over me.

I've replayed the moment a thousand times, and I still can't explain it with any word that makes sense. It wasn't desire. Not the kind I understood, not the candlelit, slow-music, consensual kind that exists in the world I'd come from. It wasn't gratitude, because you don't thank a monster for killing your friend, even when your friend deserved it. It wasn't surrender, because surrender implies giving up, and what I did next was the most active, deliberate choice I'd made all night.

It lived below thought, below language, in the place where the body makes decisions the mind refuses to make. The place where you recognize, in the bone-deep, wordless way that precedes understanding, that the thing in front of you, the terrible, monstrous, blood-soaked thing that has torn through your life like a blade through silk. Is the most honest presence you have ever encountered.

He hadn't lied to me. Not once. Not about what he was, what he wanted, what he would do. In a night defined by deception. Maya's embrace, Brian's bravado, Phoenix's smile over dinner while his phone sat face-down on the table. The Creeper was the only thing that had been exactly what it appeared to be. He'd never pretended he was safe. That was the sick part. After Phoenix, after Maya, honesty felt cleaner than kindness, even when the honest thing had claws and a mouth full of blood.

I kissed him.

He did i

Chapter Fifteen

The kiss hit hard.

His mouth was cold and rough, and the taste of copper clung to him. One hand still pinned both my wrists above my head. The wall held my back. The floor held my feet. His body took the rest of the room from me.

He did not kiss like a man. He kissed like a thing that had learned mouths from hunger. His jaw worked against mine. A low sound moved through his chest and settled under my ribs.

Under it, I found the ugliest kind of relief.

He did not lie. He did not smile while sharpening a knife behind his back. He wanted me, and he showed every tooth.

That should have terrified me more. Instead, it made a sick kind of sense. After Phoenix and Maya, honesty felt cleaner than kindness.

I broke away. My lips stung. My lungs dragged in air. Maya's blood was still drying on the bedroom floor.

"Do it." The words left my mouth before I'd decided to speak them. My voice was trembling, shaking with something that wasn't fear, or wasn't only fear, something that lived in the space between dread and desire where the two sensations overlap and become indistinguishable. "Don't stop."

Gold flared in those eyes. The color deepened, the pupils expanding, and a recognition moved behind them. An understanding that what I was offering was different from what he'd taken before. The grip on my wrists shifted. Not loosening. Releasing. Fingers uncurling, hand withdrawing, and for one suspended moment we stood face to face, untethered, unbound, two creatures in a dark hallway with nothing between them except the choice to close the distance.

He moved.

His arms found my waist and lifted me. The motion so fluid and effortless that my feet left the ground before I registered the shift in gravity. He carried me through the nearest doorway, a bedroom, dark, cold, dominated by a heavy wooden bed with a mattress that sagged in the center. He threw me —

with controlled force, strong enough to make the mattress crack beneath me but careful enough not to break me. My body hit the mattress and sank into it, the old springs groaning beneath my weight, the dust rising in a thin cloud that caught the dim light from the hallway. I landed on my back, arms spread, breath knocked loose, staring up at the cracked ceiling.

He stood in the doorway. His silhouette filled it, the wings spreading beyond the frame, the breadth of his shoulders blocking the light. He watched me for a moment that stretched longer than it should have, his chest rising and falling with controlled, deliberate breaths. Then he moved toward me. Each step was slow, measured, his bare feet silent on the floorboards. His wings rustled, old paper, pages turning in a vast and ancient book. The sound of something inevitable approaching.

I was bare. Exposed. The curtain had been torn away in the hallway, my shirt had been ripped hours ago, and I lay on the mattress with nothing between my body and the air except the dim light and his gaze. I should have covered myself. Should have crossed my arms, drawn up my knees, curled away from those eyes that tracked every line and curve of my body with the focused attention of something committing a landscape to memory.

I didn't move.

The air in the room changed as he drew closer. Warmed. Thickened. My pulse was loud in my own ears. A rapid, insistent rhythm that I could feel in my throat, in my wrists, between my legs. A heat was building inside me, deep and low, a gathering warmth that spread outward from my center in slow, pulsing waves. His dark gaze lingered on the fullness of my breasts, on the soft curve of my stomach, on the stretch marks that lined my hips — the roadmap of a pregnancy that had ended in grief — and there was no disgust in his expression. No disappointment. No averting of eyes, no polite refusal to look, no studied neutrality.

There was reverence.

He crouched between my legs. His claws traced the inside of my thighs. The tips light, barely touching, drawing lines of heat across my skin as they traveled upward. His hands were warm. The touch was deliberate, unhurried, the care of something that had time and intended to use it. He parted my legs with a grace that belied his size, gentle pressure, steady guidance, no force.

I trembled beneath his touch. Every nerve was alive,

singing, humming, vibrating at a frequency I'd never experienced. My body had responded to him before, in the ballroom, but that had been involuntary, my flesh reacting without my permission, the machinery of pleasure operating independently of consent. This was different. This was the same machinery operating with my full, terrified, willing participation.

"Please," I gasped. The word escaped before I could examine it, before I could determine whether it was a plea to stop or a plea to continue. It hung between us, ambiguous, unfinished. "Please..."

He paused. His hands rested on my thighs, motionless, the heat of his palms sinking through my skin. He looked up at me. Those dark, predatory eyes held mine, and in them I saw a question. Not the calculating assessment of a predator sizing up prey. Curiosity. Almost tenderness. As if he were trying to reconcile the woman who'd thrown a slipper at him with the one who was trembling beneath his hands and asking for more.

His gaze held mine for a long moment. Then his head dipped.

His breath reached me first, warm, uneven, brushing against the most sensitive part of me in a way that made my hips lift involuntarily. Then his mouth. His lips pressed against me, and the contact was electric, a jolt that arced through my body and made my back arch off the mattress. He was slow. Deliberate. There was no rush in how he explored me. His tongue moved with cruel patience, testing every response, catalogued every gasp, mapped the terrain of my pleasure with the patience of a cartographer charting unknown land.

The heat between us intensified with every second. My back arched, fully now, a bow of spine and muscle that lifted my hips toward him, pulling him closer, chasing what his mouth was doing to me, my thoughts dissolving into nothing but sensation. The tension inside me was a living thing, coiling, tightening, climbing higher with each stroke of his tongue, each slow, deliberate movement.

He growled against me. The sound moved through his lips and into my body, then down into my nerves, current through wire. I cried out. His grip tightened on my thighs, his claws curling without breaking skin, pressing hard enough to leave marks. Hard enough to remind me that the creature making me feel this way was not human and was not pretending to be.

I closed my eyes. Tried to hold on to something, control, composure, the last thread connecting my mind to the reality of what was happening. But my body had abandoned the effort. Every deliberate stroke, every flicker of his tongue, every vibration of his growl fed the tension building inside me, and I could feel the thread fraying, the last connection stretching, thinning, about to snap.

Warmth traveled upward. Hands leaving my thighs to trace the landscape of my body — the curve of my hip, the dip of my waist, the swell of my ribcage — until they found my breasts. Fingers curved over them, cupping, the heat of his palms pressing against skin that was already flushed and sensitive. My lungs forgot their rhythm. A soft gasp escaped, the sound of someone discovering that a body she'd spent a year hating was capable of sensations she'd forgotten existed.

Claws curled slightly, teasing the sensitive skin around my nipples. Light, circling, never quite touching the center, drawing out the anticipation until I arched into his hands, seeking the contact he was deliberately withholding. When his thumbs finally brushed across the peaks, the pleasure that shot through me was sharp enough to make me gasp and pull him closer in the same breath.

He didn't stop. His mouth continued its work — slow, torturous, relentless — while his hands explored my breasts with a possessiveness that was both terrifying and intoxicating. The dual sensation — his tongue below, his hands above — built something inside me that I couldn't fight and didn't want to. The tension climbed higher, winding tighter with each second, each touch, each vibration of his growl against me.

The orgasm arrived as something breaking.

Not a wave, a fracture. A crack that started at the center of my body and radiated outward, shattering everything it passed through. My back arched off the mattress. My muscles locked — legs, stomach, arms, jaw — every one of them seizing in the same instant. The sound I made was raw, torn from deep in my chest, a cry that had no beginning and no end, that existed only for the duration of the pleasure tearing through me.

My legs trembled. My hands gripped the mattress, fistfuls of old fabric, the seams protesting under my fingers. The waves kept coming, each one cresting and breaking, each one pulling tighter before releasing, until my body had exhausted its capacity for tension and lay shuddering in the aftermath, spent and oversensitive and still vibrating with the echo of what had passed through it.

His growl deepened. Satisfied. But he didn't stop.

I could feel him watching me through my haze, his eyes on my trembling body, his attention fixed on every aftershock. The hunger in his gaze had changed. My response fed him in some place deeper than the body. Every gasp I released became air he seemed to draw in.

He pulled back. His body rose, and for a moment he knelt

between my legs, looking down at me with an expression that I couldn't parse, too many things in it, too many layers, all of them moving at once. His chest rose and fell as though he was holding himself back, and the dim light caught the sheen of moisture on his lips, on his chin, on the angular planes of his face.

"You're beautiful."

His voice was low. Rough. The words came out like a confession held too long and released reluctantly, unpolished and true in the way that only unrehearsed words can be. He wasn't performing. He was reporting. Stating a fact as he perceived it, with the same certainty he might use to state that the sky was dark or the night was cold.

He looked at me as if nothing on my body needed correction. The gaze was heavier than a word. "All of you."

I shivered, not from cold, but from the impact of being looked at — truly looked at — by something that had no reason to lie. He wasn't talking about the version of me that fit into a plum dress for work, or the version that Phoenix paraded at business dinners, or the version that Maya's presence made feel inadequate. He was talking about THIS body, the one with the stretch marks and the soft stomach and the breasts that leaked and the hips that spread and the thighs that touched. The body I had punished and hidden and apologized for. He looked at it like it was the only thing worth looking at in the world.

No one had ever said that to me before, not while looking at all of me and meaning every word.

Rough, warm hands found my thighs, gripping with a firmness that was careful in its force. He lowered himself between my legs, and I could feel him. The heat, the mass, the proximity of something I wasn't sure I was ready for. The gaze never left mine as he positioned himself, and the look was a conversation, an exchange of information that didn't require words. I saw the question in his eyes. And he saw the answer in mine.

He tore away the leather pants in a single, fluid motion, and I gasped.

He was large. Not in the proportional, expected way of a body that scaled with its frame. Disproportionate. Intimidating in a way that made my breath catch and my body tense, the muscles in my thighs clenching involuntarily. My mind ran the calculation — size versus accommodation, force versus capacity — and the answer it returned was uncertain.

"You're mine, Rose." His voice sent a vibration through the mattress, through the frame, through the floor beneath. "All of you."

He gripped my hips. His hands were large enough to nearly span them, his fingers pressing into the soft flesh above my hipbones. Slowly — agonizingly slowly, with a control that was itself a kind of power — he pushed inside.

I cried out. My back arched off the mattress, my hands flying to his shoulders, my fingers digging into the corded muscle beneath his skin. The sensation was sharp, a stretching, a fullness that bordered on pain and then crossed the border and kept going, pushing into territory that was neither pleasure nor pain but something more fundamental than either. He filled me. Completely. In a way that made me feel every nerve ending I possessed, made me aware of the precise dimensions of my own body in a way I'd never been before.

"That's it." His voice was thick. Strained. The sound of

something exercising restraint against an instinct that wanted none. "Take all of me."

My body trembled beneath him. Every nerve was incandescent, lit up, broadcasting, the signals so intense that they'd overwhelmed the circuits designed to process them. He moved inside me, slow, deliberate, each thrust a statement rather than a motion. I could feel him everywhere. His weight pressing me into the mattress. His heat radiating through every point of contact between his body and mine. The way he filled me, withdrew, and filled me again, the rhythm steady, patient, savoring.

My breath came in short, broken gasps. My fingers dug into his shoulders, nails scraping skin that I knew wouldn't mark. I was trying to hold on to something — anything — an anchor, a fixed point in the overwhelming flood of sensation. But there was no holding on to this.

His pace quickened. The control that had defined his early thrusts loosened, replaced by a rougher need. His hips rocked against mine, and each movement drove deeper, landed harder. My legs wrapped around his waist before my mind could approve it.

I needed him deeper.

The thought arrived without permission, without precedent, without the careful vetting process that every other thought had gone through tonight. I needed him deeper, and the need was so immediate and so absolute that it overrode everything, the fear, the confusion, the moral inventory I'd been running since the basement. My hips moved in sync with his, matching each thrust, meeting each push, and the tension inside me built and built and built, a pressure that climbed past discomfort and into something that felt like standing at the edge of a high place and choosing to jump.

"Every curve," he growled. His lips were close to my ear, his breath hot and ragged. "Every inch of you." He thrust harder, and I gasped, my body arching beneath him. "Mine."

The word sent something through me that was more than physical. A shiver that started at the nape of my neck and traveled the full length of my spine. My body responded. Hips shifting, muscles tightening, the rhythm between us intensifying until the tension inside me was a solid thing, a wall I was pressed against, a surface I was about to break through.

Lips found my neck. Breath rough, uneven, the sound of something close to its own limit. The mouth moved against my skin as he spoke, each word a vibration transferred directly from his lips to my pulse point.

"Let go, Rose." A whisper. A command. A prayer. "Give it to me."

I did.

The orgasm crashed through me with a force that made the first one feel like a rehearsal. My back arched until only my shoulders and heels touched the mattress. My mouth opened. The sound that came out was something between a moan and a scream, a cry wrenched from a depth I didn't know I had. My fingers dug into his shoulders, my nails scoring his skin, my legs tightening around him with a desperate, convulsive strength. Wave after wave, each one more intense than the last, each one pulling tighter before releasing, each one drawing from a reservoir that seemed bottomless.

I was lost. Lost in the sensation. Lost in him. My body was no longer mine. It belonged to the pleasure, to the rhythm, to the creature that had caused it and was riding it with me.

His movements changed. The controlled, deliberate pace shattered, replaced by something urgent and instinctive. His hips drove against mine, faster, harder, each thrust accompanied by a growl that deepened and roughened with every second. I felt the change in his body — the tightening, the trembling, the gathering force — and when he reached his own climax, the release was a warmth that flooded through me, filling me from the inside, and the sound he made was low and broken and stripped.

He collapsed against me.

His weight settled over my body, pressing me into the mattress with a force that should have been crushing but wasn't. It was encompassing. Complete. It covered me entirely, left no part of my body exposed to the cold air, that created a barrier between me and everything else in the world. His breath came in ragged, shuddering gasps against my chest, and his wings settled around us, folded, relaxed, the membranes draping over the edges of the bed like dark curtains.

I didn't push him off. I didn't want to.

For a long moment, there was nothing. No sound except our breathing. No movement except the slow rise and fall of our chests. The room was dark and cold and smelled like dust and sweat and something metallic, but beneath his weight, wrapped in the cocoon of his wings, I was warm. Safe. A word I hadn't been able to apply to my life in over a year.

Claws — retracted now, the fingers blunt and warm — stroked my skin. Slow, aimless patterns traced across my shoulder, my arm, the curve of my waist. The touch was absent, idle, the gesture of someone too content to stop touching but too spent to have a plan. Head resting against my chest, ear pressed above my heart, and his breath was slow and even and warm.

"Nothing wasted," he murmured. The words were softer now than they'd been before, less growl, more breath, the rough edges sanded down by whatever had just passed between us. "Chosen."

I stared at the cracked ceiling. My body was still trembling, fine, residual tremors that ran through my muscles in diminishing waves. My mind was quiet. Not peaceful. That was too generous, too clean a word for what I felt. Quiet. The specific quiet of a landscape after a storm, where everything has been rearranged and you haven't yet begun the work of assessing the damage.

The room no longer felt like the place where I had almost died. It felt like a threshold. The woman who had driven to this mansion from Oklahoma, the one carrying a cooler of breast milk and a lifetime of self-doubt, the one who wore loose dresses to hide the body her husband had rejected, was receding. In her place stood someone I didn't recognize yet. Someone who had pointed at a bed and said three words. Someone who had kissed a monster. Someone who had said "don't stop" and meant it.

His head snapped up.

The motion was sudden, the lazy, post-coital stillness replaced in an instant by alert, taut focus. His body went rigid against mine, every muscle tensing, his wings twitching. His head turned toward the door, the tendons in his neck standing out. His nostrils flared. His ears — slightly pointed, set high on his skull — twitched, rotating toward a sound I couldn't detect.

His attention snapped away from me. Outside this room, outside this moment, a sound or scent had claimed priority over everything else. The warmth that had been radiating from him cooled. Not physically. Emotionally. The creature beside me was no longer the being who had murmured against my skin. He was the predator again. The hunter. Reactivated by a stimulus I couldn't perceive.

Katie. It had to be Katie.

I reached for him. My hand found his arm, the muscle taut beneath my fingers, vibrating with coiled energy. "Wait—"

But he was already moving.

His body lifted off mine in a single, powerful motion, the weight disappearing, the warmth withdrawing, the cocoon of his wings snapping open. He rose above me, his silhouette filling the ceiling of the room, those dark eyes already aimed at the doorway, already tracking something beyond it. For one suspended moment, he loomed — massive, winged, the amber light catching the planes of his face — and I saw both versions of him at once. The creature that had whispered "nothing wasted" against my skin. And the creature that had torn Sophie apart in the foyer.

Wings opened with a violent snap. The downdraft hit me, a cold, rushing blast that stripped the warmth from my skin and pressed me into the mattress. The sound of his departure was a thunderclap of displaced air, the beat of his wings carrying him through the doorway and into the dark hallway beyond, the rhythm already accelerating, already shifting from rest to pursuit.

And then he was gone. And the room was cold. And I was alone with the aftermath of what had just happened, and the knowledge of what was about to happen, and the under-standing that the only person left alive in this house who mattered to me was somewhere in the dark with a creature that had just left my bed.

ointment to me, wasn't even part of the room with a chair and that had in such my bad.

Chapter Sixteen

I grabbed the sheet from the bed and wrapped it around my body. Then I left the room.

Every step was a negotiation between my legs and the staircase. The muscles in my thighs shook with each descent, and the injured foot sent bolts of pain up through my ankle that I registered without caring about. The sheet trailed behind me, catching on the banister, dragging through the dust, and I clutched it against my chest with one hand while the other gripped the railing hard enough to whiten my knuckles.

Katie was down there. That was the only thought my mind could hold. Everything else, the sex, the aftermath, the warm weight of him against my body, what he'd murmured against my skin, was shoved into a room at the back of my skull and the door slammed shut. I couldn't afford it right now. Couldn't afford the confusion, the guilt, the bewildering tangle of emotions that would require hours of stillness to unravel. Katie was in this house, and the creature that had just left my bed was hunting.

I reached the bottom of the stairs. The hallway was dim,

the fluorescents sputtering in their death-cycle, casting everything in that same sickly, pulsing light that made shadows jump and walls seem to breathe. The air was thick. Warm in places, cold in others, the temperature layered in pockets that I walked through like curtains. And beneath the familiar smells of old wood and mildew, something else. Copper. Iron. The dense, heavy smell of blood in quantity, a catastrophe, not a wound.

I turned the corner. And the hallway opened into the space where it had happened.

Katie lay on the floor.

The Creeper stood over her, his massive frame bent forward, one clawed hand gripping her arm. She was limp, her head lolling to the side, her body crumpled like something that had been picked up and dropped from a height. A dark stain spread from her hairline down across her temple and cheek, matting her hair, pooling in the hollow of her collarbone. Her chest moved, barely. Shallow, irregular rises that came too far apart and didn't seem to pull enough air.

The wound on her head was no longer fresh, the blood already drying at the edges, the bruising darkening from red to purple. He'd hit her after Sophie. Before Alex. Before Brian. He'd struck her once, left her where she fell, and gone after the ones he wanted to destroy. Now he was back, circling, deciding whether to finish what he'd started.

He tossed her aside.

The motion was casual — a flick of his wrist, the release of his grip — and Katie's body hit the floor with a soft, heavy *thud* I felt in my teeth. She didn't move. Didn't make a sound. She lay where she landed, arms at awkward angles, her face pressed against the floorboards, and the only sign that she was

171

still alive was the faint, stuttering fog of her breath against the dust.

My gaze moved beyond her. I didn't want it to. My eyes traveled the length of the hallway against my will, pulled by the same compulsion that makes you look at a wreck on the highway. The need to see, even when seeing will cost you something you can't get back.

Alex lay against the far wall. What was left of him. His body had been opened, the torso split, the ribs visible, pale and wet in the fluorescent light. His face was turned toward me, and his eyes were open, fixed on a point somewhere past the ceiling, past the house, past anything the living could reach. The expression on his face was not pain, it was surprise. As if the last thing he'd felt before dying was disbelief that this was how it ended. Beside him — around him — pieces of what had been inside him were scattered across the floor in dark, glistening arrangements that my brain refused to catalog.

Brian was farther down the hall. I could only identify him by his shoes, the rest of him had been worked over with a thoroughness that went beyond feeding into something personal. The Creeper had taken his time with Brian. The evidence of it was everywhere. On the walls, on the floor, in the streaks and smears that told the story of a body being systematically dismantled while it was still capable of feeling it.

My stomach lurched. A wave of nausea rolled through me, hot and violent, and I pressed my hand against my mouth, swallowing hard, forcing the bile back down. My eyes burned. My legs trembled. The smell — God, the smell — was in my nose, my mouth, my clothes, and it was the smell of people I knew, people whose names I could say, people who had been alive four hours ago.

The Creeper turned back to Katie. His claws flexed, extending, the curved tips catching the light. He crouched over her, one hand finding her shoulder, the other rising above her in a position I recognized. The position that preceded the strike. The wind-up. The moment before the claw descended and ended whatever breath was still cycling through her body.

"No!"

The scream ripped out of me before I could think it. Raw, ragged, carrying every ounce of air in my lungs, the sound bouncing off the walls and the ceiling and the blood-slicked floor. My legs moved, not running, just stumbling forward, the sheet tangling around my ankles, my injured foot screaming.

The Creeper's head snapped toward me. His hand froze mid-rise, the claws suspended above Katie's body, motionless. Those gold eyes locked onto mine, and for a second the predatory focus held, the hunger, the instinct, the ancient programming that told him to finish what he'd started.

Then the hunger left his face.

He straightened. His hand lowered. His body moved away from Katie. Not retreating, exactly, but redirecting, his attention pivoting from the unconscious woman on the floor to the one standing in the hallway doorway, barefoot, wrapped in a stained sheet, with tears she couldn't stop running down her face.

He moved toward me. Not the ceiling-crawl from earlier, not the blurred lunge that had killed Sophie. He dropped to all fours and approached at a measured, deliberate pace, the movement of something large and powerful choosing to make itself slow. His shadow reached me before he did, stretching across the floor, swallowing my feet, my legs, my body in a darkness that seemed to have more substance than the light it displaced.

He loomed over me. His massive frame blocked everything else, the hallway, the bodies, the flickering lights. The air between us was thick, heated by his proximity, and his breath moved across my face, my forehead, my cheeks, the wet tracks of my tears.

Then he did something I didn't expect.

He reached out. His hand — those claws that had torn through Sophie, through Alex, through Brian — extended toward my face. And with a gentleness that had no right to exist in the same creature that had committed the horrors behind him, his claw brushed my cheek. The touch was feather-light. Precise. The curved tip tracing the path of a tear from the hollow beneath my eye to the edge of my jaw, collecting the moisture on its surface, wiping it away.

The contrast was so violent — the tenderness of his touch against the carnage at his back — that something in my chest broke open. A crack, not a sob. The sound a dam makes when the water behind it has been building too long.

"Please." My voice was a fractured thing, held together by nothing. "Don't hurt her."

He stilled. His hand remained at my cheek, the claw resting against my jaw. His head tilted — a slow, birdlike rotation — and his eyes narrowed with assessment. The focused, calculating attention of something processing new information and trying to determine its significance.

When he spoke, the sound came from everywhere, his mouth, the floor, the walls, the air itself, a resonance that bypassed my ears and went directly into my chest, vibrating in my ribcage, a struck bell. His lips moved, but the voice that emerged was larger than the motion that produced it. Deep. Grinding. Each word pulled from a depth that suggested the act of speaking required effort, the effort of translation, of compressing thoughts that existed in a language older than sound into shapes my human ears could recognize.

"You beg for her life." The words settled between us, stones dropped into still water, heavy, concentric ripples spreading outward from each one. "But what has she ever done for you?"

I blinked. The question landed with a dissonance that made my brain stutter, like a familiar sound played at the wrong speed, enough to make you doubt your own hearing. He was speaking. The creature — the Creeper — was using words. Forming sentences. Asking questions with the structure and cadence of something that understood language well enough to wield it.

"You can talk?" The question fell out of me, unformed, incredulous.

His face shifted — not quite a smile, too asymmetric and too brief — but a rearrangement of features that suggested amusement occupying a face not designed to express it. His lips pulled back at one corner, exposing the edge of a tooth. His eyes crinkled, the faintest contraction of the skin around them, barely visible in the dim light.

"I've walked this earth longer than you can comprehend." His voice scraped low, the words delivered with a flatness that bordered on contempt for the question. As if the assumption that he couldn't speak was an insult so minor it was barely worth correcting. "Of course I can speak." He paused. The half-smile faded. "But it's a waste on most."

The last four words carried more weight than they should

have. *A waste on most.* The implication was clear: most of the people he encountered weren't worth the effort of speaking to. They were food. Resources. Bodies to be consumed, not communicated with. The fact that he was speaking to me, that he was standing here, forming words, answering questions instead of finishing what he'd started with Katie, meant something. I wasn't sure what. But it meant something.

I swallowed. My gaze darted past him — past his shoulder, past the shadow of his wings — to where Katie lay on the floor. Her head was bleeding. The stain had spread, darkening the boards beneath her, and the sight of it was a fist around my lungs.

"Leave her." The words came out in a whisper, cracked at the seams. "Please. Just leave her alone."

He stopped directly in front of me. His body cast a shadow that swallowed me whole, atmospherically, the air in his shadow colder, denser, carrying a charge that made the fine hairs on my arms stand straight. His glowing eyes narrowed, and something crossed his expression that I could only describe as consideration. As if my request was an equation he was working through, balancing variables I couldn't see.

"And if I refuse?"

My stomach knotted. The question wasn't rhetorical. He was asking, not taunting. The question you ask someone who has offered a trade: what are they willing to put on the table. The realization that there was a negotiation happening, that the creature standing over the body of my friend was waiting for a counteroffer, made the room tilt beneath my feet.

He began to move, around me, not toward Katie. A slow, circling orbit, his body shifting in the dim light, his wings folded tight, his claws clicking softly against the floor with each step. The motion was predatory in form but not in intent. He wasn't hunting me. He was studying me. Evaluating me from every angle, a jeweler turning a stone through the light.

"When I take them," he murmured, the words dropping lower, the resonance thinning to something closer to a murmur, intimate and dangerous, "I take more than just their lives." He completed half the circle and paused behind me. I could feel his breath on the back of my neck, warm and measured. "Blood. Flesh. Fear." He was in front of me again, close enough that I could see the striations in his irises. "Each one tells me something different. What people bury deepest, what they've done, what they've carried."

The air had been pulled from the room. There was nothing left to breathe. Only the thick, compressed atmosphere between his body and mine, charged with the truth he was unspooling one word at a time.

"I know what they've done to you." He tilted his head, those gold eyes searching my face. "I tasted you in that field." His eyes held mine. "Your milk, your fear. Your grief was already in you when I found you. What they'd done, what they'd hidden. I read that from their blood, after. Phoenix was only a name carried inside your fear."

The sentence hit me in the chest, in the exact cage of bone that held everything broken by the people who had claimed to love me. The Creeper wasn't guessing. He wasn't reading my face. He knew. He had fed on the people who hurt me, and their secrets had passed into him with their blood.

A sob tore out of me. The crying tore out of me, the kind that contorts your face and tears loose sounds that belong to no emotional vocabulary you've been taught. The tears came with it. The full, racking kind that pull your shoulders forward and make you fold in on yourself like paper being crumpled.

He was right. He was absolutely, devastatingly, unbearably right. Maya's cruelty. Brian's contempt. Phoenix's cold, systematic dismantling of everything I thought I was. All of it rushed back as sensation, the physical experience of being diminished, betrayed, abandoned, reduced to a body that wasn't good enough, a wife that wasn't thin enough, a friend that wasn't worth protecting. The Creeper stood in front of me and watched the wreckage pour out, and his expression held no pity. No sympathy. Just recognition.

Claws brushed my arm. Light. Careful. The touch traveling from my shoulder to my elbow in a slow, descending line that left warmth in its wake.

"But you..." The word was heavier. Laden with something I couldn't identify. "You are different."

I looked up at him through the blur of tears. His face was close. Those gold eyes held mine with an intensity that went beyond hunger, beyond predation, into a space I had no map for.

"You don't hide like they do." The words came rough, each one scraped over gravel. "You feel everything." His hand — still on my arm, the claws barely touching — tightened fractionally. "It makes you open." He leaned closer. His breath was warm against my face. "It makes you *real*."

The words found the place I'd been walling off for years and broke straight through. The place where I kept the belief that feeling everything was a weakness, that the depth of my grief and the naked heat of my anger made me too much, too needy, too overwhelming for anyone to want. Phoenix had told me that. Maya had confirmed it. Brian had mocked it. And now a creature that had walked the earth for longer than I could comprehend was standing in a blood-soaked hallway and telling me that the thing everyone else had punished me for was the thing that made me worth speaking to.

"You looked at the dark," he murmured, his lips barely moving, the words more breath than sound. His eyes searched my face with an attention that was almost painful in its focus. "And stepped closer."

The dam broke.

I threw my arms around him. The motion was artless, graceless, a lunge more than an embrace, my body crashing into his with a force that surprised us both. My arms wrapped around his torso, my face buried against his chest, and the sob that came out of me was something older than grief or fear, more fundamental, the sound of a person who had been holding herself upright for so long that the muscles had forgotten how to let go, and was finally, violently, completely letting go.

The Creeper stiffened. His body went rigid beneath my arms, every muscle taut, his wings flaring slightly, the reflex of something unaccustomed to contact that wasn't violent. For two full seconds, he didn't move.

Then his arms wrapped around me. Slowly. His massive hands found my back, his claws retracting as they settled against my skin, and he pulled me in. The embrace was awkward, his body wasn't shaped for this, wasn't designed for tenderness, the proportions wrong, the angles uncomfortable. But the intention behind it was unmistakable. He was holding me, not restraining. Holding.

I hated myself for needing comfort while Katie was still bleeding somewhere in this house. But I took it anyway. I cried into his chest. Ugly, wrenching sobs that soaked the skin beneath my face and made my body shake against his. He held me through it. He held me without letting go, his arms tight, his breathing slow and even against the top of my head. He didn't speak. He didn't need to.

When the worst of it had passed, when the sobs had thinned to hitching breaths and the tears had slowed to a trickle, he shifted. His arms loosened, adjusting rather than releasing. And without a word, he began to move.

Chapter Seventeen

He led me through the mansion. His hand found mine — claws retracted, fingers rough and warm — and he guided me through corridors I'd run through in terror hours ago. Past the living room. Past the foyer, where Sophie's blood had dried to a dark stain on the tile. Down, into the belly of the house, into the basement where Katie and Alex and I had found the fuse box and the book and the door marked *Creatura Noctis*.

As we descended, I saw it, the Codex Arcanum, still lying where Alex had dropped it, its leather cover splayed open on the dirt floor. The pages had fanned out, yellowed and brittle, covered in symbols I couldn't read. A book that had tried to warn us. A book we hadn't stayed long enough to understand. It would burn with everything else, I thought. And maybe that was right.

He stopped at the door. His free hand pressed against it, and the old wood swung inward with a low, grinding groan.

The stench hit me like a wall. Sharp, metallic, suffocating, the concentrated smell of death compressed into a small space and left to ripen. Every breath I drew tasted like iron and decay, thick and foul, coating the inside of my mouth and clinging to the back of my throat. My lungs rejected it — the reflex to stop breathing kicking in before I could override it — and I pressed my free hand against my nose and mouth, my eyes watering.

The floor was slick. Cold and wet beneath my bare feet, the surface coated with things I didn't want to name. I could feel them, textures that were too varied, too organic, too wrong to be anything but the residue of what had happened in this room over years, decades, centuries. This room wasn't on any floor plan. It opened only when the house wanted someone to find it. Small things crunched beneath my steps, brittle, snapping sounds that traveled up through the soles of my feet and into my ankles. Bones. Small and old and fragile, ground into the floor by the weight of time and new additions.

The bulb burned without power, fed by something older than wires, its light wrong-gold and sputtering. Each flash revealed a new detail, each pause between flashes mercifully hid it again. But I saw enough.

Skulls. Ribs. Limbs, mangled, disjointed, suspended from rusted chains that hung from the low ceiling like grotesque ornaments. Some still had flesh, dried, darkened, clinging to the bone in papery strips. Others were fresh. Too fresh. The blood on them still wet, the skin still holding color, the identity of their owners still readable in the shapes of their faces.

Scattered among the bones were remnants of the living. A shoe, small, feminine, the leather cracked with age. A watch, its face clouded, the hands stopped at a time that no longer mattered. A pair of glasses, one lens shattered, the frame bent. The personal effects of people who had come to this place and never left, their possessions outlasting them, persisting in this room, headstones in a graveyard without graves.

My stomach heaved. I pressed my hand harder against my mouth, my body convulsing with the effort of not vomiting. My legs shook. My vision blurred. Every inch of this room screamed with the evidence of what had been done here, and the screams were silent and old and had been going on for longer than I could imagine.

The Creeper stood beside me. His dark eyes glowed faintly in the flickering light, watching me take it in. And on his face. An expression I hadn't expected. The look of a creature showing the rot under its own ribs. The look of someone showing you the part of themselves they've kept hidden, because the moment demands it. The look of something that knows what it is and has decided to stop pretending.

"This is what I am." His voice was gravelly, nearly lost beneath the hum of the dying bulb. The words were simple. Declarative. Offered without defense or apology.

I swallowed hard. Forced my hand away from my mouth. Forced my eyes to stay open, to keep looking at the room, at the evidence, at the creature standing in the middle of it. "Why?" The word trembled in the air. "Why do you do this? Why them?"

He tilted his head. His wings shifted, a subtle adjustment, the membranes rustling against his back. He stepped closer, his claws brushing one of the hanging skulls as he passed, a light, almost absent touch, the gesture of someone moving through a familiar space.

"I feed on their bodies, their fear." His tone was flat, declarative. "It's what sustains me."

"How?" The question was thin and unsteady.

He met my gaze. The half-smile returned, faint, sardonic, carrying centuries behind his teeth. "I wasn't made for your world, Rose." He paced the room slowly, his clawed hand dragging along the stone wall, the tips leaving thin white lines in the grime. "I'm not human. Never was."

He stopped. Turned. His eyes found mine across the room, and the distance between us felt vast and intimate at the same time.

"I come from a place with no name." The words ground out of him. "Older than your gods. Where I come from, there is only hunger." His lips thinned. "Things like me, clawing for survival."

The room was silent except for the buzz of the bulb and the faint drip of something I didn't want to identify. He paced again, his shadow sweeping the walls.

"Any form." He looked down at himself — the grayish-green skin, the dark veins, the claws — and there was no pride in it. Only recognition. "This is the one that fits."

His eyes were darker now, the gold pulled back to a thin ring around expanding black. He turned toward me, each step closing the distance with the unhurried certainty of something that had all the time in the world.

"The hunger never stops." He stopped an arm's length away. "Every day it gnaws. Most of the time I can hold it." His hands curled at his sides, claws extending and retracting once, involuntary. "But Halloween. It's as if the place I came from pulls at me. Wakes something I can't suppress."

"I try to curb it." His breath was warm on my face, uneven. "But on that night, the hunger always wins. If I don't feed, I rot. I lose myself. I become something worse." A pause that had weight to it. "That's why I hunt. Why I kill."

I let the words settle and looked at him. At what it had cost him. The creature that had torn through this house was standing in the evidence of centuries, showing me all of it, because I'd asked.

I swallowed. Forced myself to hold his gaze. Forced the next question past the tightness in my throat.

"Then why didn't you kill me?"

He stepped closer. Close enough that I could feel the heat radiating from his skin, the unnatural warmth of a body that ran hotter than human, the proximity of something massive and ancient and dangerous standing inches away and choosing — for reasons I didn't yet understand — not to be dangerous.

The lips curled. Slow. Deliberate. The dark smile of something that had been waiting for this question.

"I fed on you." The words came low, intimate, pitched for an audience of one. "Your milk. Your essence." His eyes dropped to my chest, the briefest glance, weighted with memory. "It's unlike anything I've ever tasted." He drew a breath. Deep, slow, as if the memory of the taste was enough to trigger the physical response of savoring it. "Pure. Powerful." His eyes returned to mine. "It gave me strength. Sustenance, like nothing else in all the centuries I've walked."

A shiver ran through me, starting at the base of my skull and traveling the full length of my spine, branching outward through my shoulders, my arms, my fingers. The thing I had been ashamed of. The thing that woke me at 4 a.m. and kept me buying nursing pads and forced me to wear scarves and stand sideways and pump in dark rooms. The thing that marked me as a mother without a child, a body stuck in a function that had no purpose.

That was what sustained him. That was what set me apart

from every other person he'd consumed in this house, in this century, in all the centuries before. Not my beauty, not my personality, not the things people usually measure worth by. My milk. The biological accident of a body that hadn't stopped lactating after a pregnancy that ended in blood on a kitchen floor.

The thing that made me broken was the thing that made me sacred to him.

Chapter Eighteen

My mouth opened and nothing came. My lungs had emptied and wouldn't refill.

Your milk. Your essence. Unlike anything I've ever tasted. His words stayed in the bone room the way the bones did. They belonged there. And so, it turned out, did I.

My body. The body that woke me at four in the morning with its aching. The body that stained my shirts and soaked through nursing pads and forced me to carry a cooler of milk to a bank where strangers' babies would drink what my dead baby never could. The body that Phoenix had called a whale. The body that didn't fit into the plum dress, that Katie complimented out of kindness, that Brian leered at out of cruelty, that Maya never once mentioned because acknowledging it would have meant acknowledging what she'd helped destroy.

That body was the reason I was alive. Not my personality or my beauty, not the things people evaluate and rank and assign worth to. My milk. The most intimate, most shameful, most relentlessly persistent reminder of the worst thing that had ever happened to me, the pregnancy that ended in blood on a kitchen floor, the baby that never drew breath, the marriage that decomposed while the breast pump hummed in the dark.

That was what sustained him. That was what no one else had ever given him. That was what made me, among all the living things he had consumed across all the centuries he had walked, different.

My knees softened. The strength that had carried me through the hallways and down the stairs and into this room was failing, gradually, like a battery draining, each system shutting down in sequence. My hands trembled at my sides. My breath came in shallow, unsteady pulls. The sheet around my body felt too thin, too loose, the fabric a barrier so flimsy it might as well not exist.

"If I give it to you willingly."

The words came slow. Each one chosen separately, placed in the air with the care of someone laying stones across a river, testing each one before committing weight to it. My voice shook. Not from fear. From the magnitude of what I was offering, and the understanding that once the offer was made, there was no taking it back.

"If I give you what you want..." I swallowed. My eyes found his. Held them. "Will you stop?" The question came out smaller than I intended, the final word barely more than a breath that shaped itself into meaning. "Will you spare her?"

The gold in his eyes flared and dimmed, pupils contracting and expanding in rapid succession, a system recalibrating, processing input that didn't match existing categories. Hunger was there. It never left. The hunger was a permanent feature of his face, present in the set of his jaw, the flare of his nostrils, the way his tongue moved behind his teeth when he was close to something he wanted. But now it was joined by bewilderment. The expression a person makes when they hear a word in a language they thought they'd forgotten.

"You would give that..." His voice was quieter than before. The resonance diminished, the authority softened, the centuries-old confidence replaced by something thinner and more fragile. "For her?" A pause. His eyes searched my face. "For your friend?"

I shook my head. The motion was small but definite, a correction, not a denial. "Not just for her." My voice dropped. Steadied. Found a register I didn't know I possessed, calm, clear, coming from a place below the fear and the grief, from the bedrock of something I'd only just discovered was there. "But because I *want* to give it to you."

The last six words changed the air.

I could feel it, a physical shift, as if the room had inhaled and was holding its breath. The chains above us stopped swaying. The drip in the corner paused. Even the flickering bulb seemed to steady, its cycle interrupted by the weight of what I'd said.

Because I want to give it to you.

This was not a transaction. This was not an exchange, my milk for Katie's life, one commodity traded for another. This was communion. The word "gift" was too small to contain it. I was offering him the thing that had cost me the most, the thing that woke me every night, that reminded me every morning of what I'd lost. And I was offering it because recognition demanded expression. My body recognized his hunger. His hunger recognized my grief. The only honest expression was this.

He blinked.

The motion was slow. Deliberate. His eyelids descending and rising with the conscious control of someone blinking on purpose, buying time, the one-second darkness behind his eyes a space in which to process something that has exceeded his capacity to process in the light. When his eyes opened, they were different. The hunger was still present, it would always be present, it was structural, woven into the architecture of what he was. But it was no longer alone.

Confusion. I saw it first. The specific confusion of something encountering a phenomenon it has no framework for, categorical failure, the inability to assign what it's witnessing to any existing box. His brow furrowed. His head tilted. The half-smile that had been his default expression all night disappeared, replaced by something open and uncertain.

Then awe. It moved across his face like weather crossing a landscape, visible in the changing light, in the shifting planes, in the way his jaw loosened and his lips parted and his chest expanded with a breath that was deeper and slower than any he'd drawn before. He was looking at me the way the old man in my flower shop had looked at the roses he was buying for his wife, as if the thing in front of him was so far beyond what he'd expected to find that the discovery itself was a kind of wound.

He stepped back. The motion was involuntary. I could tell by the way his body moved, the slight stagger, the wings adjusting for balance. His massive frame, which had filled every room he'd entered with the authority of something that had never been surprised, faltered. The faltering was visible in his shoulders, in the slight hitch of his breathing, in the way his hands opened at his sides. Claws extending and retracting, extending and retracting, a nervous tic I hadn't seen before.

Tears.

They arrived without announcement. No sound preceded them, no contortion of his face, no intake of breath. They simply appeared, welling in the dark centers of his eyes, gathering along the lower lids, growing heavy, trembling, and then spilling over. Two lines of moisture traced down his face, following the angular geometry of his cheekbones, catching the flickering light and shining briefly before disappearing into the rough terrain of his jaw.

He wept silently. The tears fell, and his face held still, and the contrast between the two — the motion of the tears and the stillness of everything else — was devastating. He looked like a statue being rained on. A thing made of stone that had somehow learned to grieve.

He dropped to his knees.

The impact was heavy, the full weight of his body, the density of bone and muscle and centuries, hitting the stone floor with a sound that resonated through the room and up through my bare feet and into the base of my spine. The chains above us swayed. The dust on the floor jumped and resettled. He knelt in front of me, his body folding, his wings collapsing behind him, and his arms found my waist and wrapped around it with a desperation that I felt in my own chest.

He pulled me close. His head pressed against my stomach, the side of his face flat against the sheet, his ear above my navel, his arms cinched around my hips. The grip was fierce, almost desperate, like he'd found the one thing he needed and already feared losing it. His body shook against me, fine tremors running through his shoulders, his arms, the muscles of his back.

"Why?" The word was muffled against my body, thick

with an emotion that his voice hadn't been built to express. He pressed closer, his grip tightening, his face buried against me. "Why would you do this..." He drew a shuddering breath. "...for a monster like me?"

The question broke something open in me that I didn't know was closed.

My hands found his head. My fingers threaded into his hair, coarse, thick, warm beneath my touch. I curled my hands through it, cradling his skull against my body, feeling the shape of him, the ridges, the heat, the pulse of something ancient beating beneath the bone. My own tears came, a steady fall this time that ran down my cheeks and dripped onto the top of his head.

"Because," I murmured. My breath was shaky. My voice was not. The words came from the place below the fear, the place I'd discovered minutes ago and was still learning to speak from. "Phoenix told me he loved me every day for three years, and he was lying every time. Maya texted me sympathy while I lay in that hospital bed. And she was the reason I was in it." I swallowed. My fingers tightened in his hair. "You tore people apart in front of me tonight. And you're the only one who never pretended to be something you weren't." The sentence was absurd. I knew it was absurd. I was standing in a room hung with human remains, cradling the head of the creature that had put them there, and I was telling him I trusted his honesty more than any human's kindness. But the absurdity of it was the point. The trust wasn't logical. It was true. "With you, I feel safe." I exhaled. "In some fucked-up way."

His grip around my waist tightened, completely, his arms drawing me closer with the focused strength of something that was holding on to the only solid thing in an otherwise formless existence. His body trembled against mine, the shaking intensi-fying before gradually subsiding, the pattern of a wave cresting and breaking and pulling back.

He lifted his face. His wet eyes lifted to mine from below, the flickering light caught in two points of gold. The disbelief was still there. The awe. But there was trust, new and unsteady, not the easy, reflexive trust of someone who hasn't been hurt, but the careful, tentative trust of something that has been hurt so many times and so thoroughly that the act of trusting again requires more courage than the act of killing.

Cracked, rough lips found my right palm. A kiss so light it was almost a breath given shape. He held the contact for a moment, his mouth warm against my skin, then moved to my wrist. Another kiss. Soft. Reverent. The motion had the quality of ritual. Each point of contact a station in a ceremony I didn't know the rules of but could feel the pull of.

He worked his way up my arm. Wrist to forearm. Forearm to inner elbow. Inner elbow to the soft skin above, where the vein showed blue beneath the surface. Each kiss was deliber-ate, unhurried, placed with a precision that suggested he was marking territory with tenderness, not claiming but conse-crating.

Through every press of his lips, every breath against my skin, those eyes never left mine, reading my reaction, regis-tering every flutter of my eyelids, every catch of my breath, every micro-expression that crossed my face. The attention was total. Overwhelming. The focused devotion of something that had found an object worthy of worship and was performing the first act of its new religion.

"Rose." He said my name. The sound of it in his mouth was different from any other time I'd heard it, rough, broken, carrying a weight that the two syllables weren't designed to bear. The name I'd been given at birth, that had been printed on divorce papers and medical records and the sign above a flower shop, became something else when he said it. An invocation. A prayer directed at the thing it named.

Chapter Nineteen

I lowered myself into his lap.

My legs wrapped around his waist, my knees settling against his hips, my body pressed against the broad, warm expanse of his chest. His heartbeat was erratic, fast, uneven, pounding against my sternum with a rhythm that had no pattern, the cardiac equivalent of speech that couldn't find words. My hands found his shoulders, wide, corded with muscle, the skin warm and rough beneath my palms.

The gaze traced my face. Slowly. Thoroughly. Reading me the way you read a passage you want to memorize, dwelling on each feature as if photographing it for permanent storage. Hands came to rest on my waist, fingers spread, claws retracted, the touch careful and warm and trembling with the effort of restraint. He was holding me the way you hold something fragile, because the thought of breaking it is unbearable.

I leaned in. My lips brushed his ear. My breath was warm against the skin there. I could feel him shiver, could feel the muscles in his neck tighten and release.

"Take what you need," I whispered. The words were

steady. Sure. Given freely, without condition, without the shadow of transaction. Not *take this and spare Katie*. Not *take this and I'll forgive you*. Just: take. What you need. From me.

He shuddered. The tremor ran through his entire body, starting at his core and radiating outward through his limbs, his wings, the tips of his claws. His eyes closed. His teeth set. The muscles in his neck stood out as he swallowed against something that was rising in his throat, a sound, an emotion, a response too large for the apparatus designed to express it.

Then, with a slowness that bordered on ceremony, he leaned forward.

His head descended toward my chest. No diving, no lunging, none of the frenzied hunger from the ballroom. This was deliberate. Liturgical. Each inch of descent was a conscious choice, to approach slowly, to give me the time and space to change my mind, to arrive at the point of contact having traveled the full distance with his eyes open and his intentions exposed.

A mouth found my breast.

Lips parted against my skin, warm, slightly rough, the pressure tentative at first, testing. I felt breath first, a warm, unsteady gust that raised gooseflesh across my chest and made my nipple tighten. Then his lips closed around it, and he drew the first pull, and the sensation that moved through me was unlike anything I had words for.

I gasped. My body trembled, a full-system response, every nerve firing simultaneously. His hands tightened on my waist, pulling me closer, the motion instinctive, the grip reflecting a need that went beyond the physical. The heat of his mouth, the soft pressure of his lips, the slow, rhythmic pull. It was intimate in a way that transcended the sexual, that reached past the body and into some deeper territory where the boundaries between feeding and nurturing, between taking and giving, between hunger and love became impossible to distinguish.

Each pull was deliberate. Slow. Measured. He drew from me with the unhurried care of someone who has been given access to something precious and is determined not to waste a drop, not to rush, not to let the experience blur into haste. My milk flowed, and he drank, and the rhythm between us settled into something steady and ancient, the oldest rhythm in the world, the one that connects the body that gives to the body that receives, the one that predates language and thought and every complicated structure humans have built on top of the simple act of nourishment.

The tongue moved against my nipple, slow, circling, the pressure light, the touch more caress than feeding. I whimpered. The sound escaped without my permission, pulled from a place I hadn't known was sensitive to this. The fact that I was choosing this, that my body was doing what it was designed to do, that the function I'd been punishing myself for was, in this moment, being received with reverence.

My fingers threaded deeper into his hair. I cupped the back of his skull, pressing him closer, feeling the motion of his jaw against my breast, the warmth of his mouth, the slight vibration of each swallow traveling through his throat and into my body. The connection was total. Every point of contact between us was conducting something, heat, need, the unnameable current that ran between a body offering sustenance and a body receiving it.

He moaned. The sound was soft, nearly inaudible, a vibration more than a vocalization, traveling through his lips into my breast and resonating through my ribcage. The moan carried centuries of hunger in it, and beneath the hunger, something more fragile: gratitude. Relief. The specific, devastating relief of something that has been starving for longer than memory and has finally been fed by choice rather than by force.

I moaned in response. My hand pressed him closer, my back arching, my breath catching in my throat. My nipple was swollen and tender from his mouth. Every flick of his tongue, every gentle graze of his teeth, every pull of his lips sent waves of pleasure through me. This pleasure was warmer than the bedroom. It came from being needed. From being the answer to a need that had existed for centuries before I was born.

He drew from me, and my body stopped feeling like proof of loss.

"Creeper." I whispered his name against his ear. The breath barely carried it, the word more vibration than sound, a secret passed between bodies in contact.

His entire body tightened. The muscles in his back went rigid, his wings flared slightly, his arms pulled me flush against him until there was no space left. A shiver ran through him, visible, violent, starting at the base of his spine and traveling upward. His breath turned ragged against my skin, his mouth stuttering in its rhythm, his hands sliding up my back with a desperation that made my own breath catch.

The sound of his name had changed him in a way the centuries hadn't prepared him for. He'd been called many things, monster, creature, beast, Creatura Noctis, the thing in the dark. Nobody had called him by name. Nobody had whispered it against his skin while he drank from them. Nobody had made the name sound like what I'd made it sound like.

The moment stretched. Thinned. Became something

translucent, fragile, holding more weight than it should have been able to bear. His mouth continued to draw from me, slower now, the rhythm winding down, the pulls becoming gentler, less urgent, more lingering, the feeding transforming into something closer to touch, to communion, to the simple act of staying connected for as long as possible.

He pulled back.

A soft, wet sound, release. The mouth left me and the head tilted upward, eyes finding mine, and the expression on his face was the most unguarded thing I had ever seen on any face, human or otherwise. Wide eyes. Glossy. Reflecting my face back to me in miniature, two small images of myself in the wet dark of his irises. Lips — swollen, glistening, parted — trembling. A soft gasp escaped him, involuntary, the sound of someone surfacing from water they'd been held beneath for too long.

He looked at me as though I'd changed the terms of his existence. The act of giving — freely, willingly, without coercion — had introduced a variable into an equation that had been running the same answer for centuries. He didn't know what to do with it. The not-knowing was written across his face in the language of bewilderment, the lines around his eyes deepening, his brow creasing, his mouth working silently around words that hadn't been invented yet.

My fingers found his face. I brushed the hair back from his forehead, the strands damp, clinging to his skin. My thumb traced the line of his cheekbone, feeling the wetness of the tears that had dried there, the rough texture of skin that had endured centuries of weather and violence and loneliness.

"You never pretended you weren't one," I whispered.

He closed his eyes. His forehead dropped against my chest,

heavy, surrendering, the weight of his skull pressing against me with the trust of something that had lowered its guard completely. A tremor ran through him. Deep. Sustained. His arms tightened around me with a fierceness that spoke of desperation. The grip of something that had been given a reprieve it hadn't asked for and was afraid to believe was real.

A sound came from him. A sound between a growl and a moan. A laugh, short, dry, carrying no joy. The mirthless exhalation of something that finds the universe's cruelest irony directed at itself.

"You see the good in people," he rasped against my chest. His breath was warm through the sheet, through my skin, down into the cage of my ribs. "Even in monsters." A pause. "Why?"

The answer was in my mouth before my mind had shaped it. "Because I spent a year being invisible." My fingers moved through his hair, slow, rhythmic, the motion automatic, the gesture maternal in a way that made my chest ache with the terrible irony of it: a woman without a child comforting a creature that had killed her friends. "To my husband. To my friend. To everyone who looked at me and decided I wasn't worth seeing." My hand stilled on his temple. "You looked at me tonight and saw everything. The milk, the grief, the anger, all of it. You're the first one who didn't look away."

He was quiet for a moment. Then his grip loosened, shifting, his head turning so his words pressed directly into the skin above my sternum.

"Fear sharpens me," he murmured, the words vibrating against my chest. "Flesh keeps me whole." A pause. The arms tightened again. "What you gave me did what flesh never could. It held me here." Another breath, slower, measured. "No one has ever given willingly. It changed the door. It changed the hunger. I don't understand it yet. But it changed."

The room was quiet. The bulb had stopped flickering. Whether it had steadied or died completely, I couldn't tell. The air had settled. The chains above us hung motionless. Even the persistent drip in the corner had stopped, as if the room itself was holding still.

He didn't move for a long time. His forehead against my chest. His arms around me. His breathing slow and deep and steady, each exhale warm against my skin. I held him. My hands in his hair, my body cradling his head, the sheet pooled around my waist, the cold of the room a distant fact that couldn't penetrate the warmth between us.

Then, slowly, he lifted his head.

The gold in his eyes stayed warm, like embers banked for the night. He searched my face. Whatever he found there seemed to settle something in him, a decision reached, a door opened or closed.

Without a word, he pulled me into him. His arms wrapped around me, fully, completely, his hands on my back, his wings curling forward to enclose us both in a canopy of dark membrane that blocked the light and the room and the bones. Inside that shelter, there was only warmth, and his heartbeat, and the sound of two breathing patterns slowly synchronizing.

The thought arrived like a hand closing around my throat.

Katie.

I stiffened. The change was immediate, my muscles locking, my breath catching, my body rigid in his arms. The warmth that had insulated me — the cocoon of wings and breath and connection — thinned, and through it came the cold reality of the house above us, and the woman lying on the floor somewhere in it, bleeding from her head, her breath shallow and uneven.

I pulled away. His arms resisted with the reluctant loosening of something that didn't want to let go but recognized it had to. I leaned back far enough to see his face, my hands on his shoulders, my eyes searching his.

"Katie." The name came out cracked, weighted with everything I was asking. "She's good." My voice was thick. Urgent. "My best friend. She doesn't deserve this."

Dark, layered eyes found mine. The expression behind them was complex, too many things happening at once to parse individually. I could see the predator in there, the ancient, hungry thing that fed because it had to and killed because the alternative was worse. But I could see the other thing too, the thing that had wept, that had pressed its face against my stomach, that had whispered *why* with a rough, broken cadence thick with disbelief.

"She's everything good," I whispered. My hands tightened on his shoulders. "You don't have to hurt her." The words were running out, each one smaller than the last, carrying less certainty, more plea. "Please."

His body tensed. The muscles beneath my hands went rigid, a response I'd seen before, the physical signature of a creature wrestling with its own nature. A muscle leapt in his cheek. His nostrils flared. His eyes held mine, and behind the gold I could see the conflict, the hunger that never stopped, that gnawed every moment, that on this night of all nights surged beyond the boundaries of control. Fighting against something newer, something that had been planted in the bone room when I'd said *because I want to give it to you* and was growing now, sending roots into the bedrock of his oldest instincts.

For a moment — a long, suspended, terrible moment — I thought he would refuse. His shoulders squared. His eyes hardened. The predator surfaced, old and cold and certain, and I could feel the answer forming in his body before it reached his mouth.

Then something softened.

It moved through him like a sigh, a visible release of tension, a loosening of the coiled, compressed energy that had held his body taut. His jaw unclenched. His shoulders dropped. His eyes, which had hardened to amber stone, warmed, slowly, degree by degree, the way ice melts under sustained contact with something warm.

His grip on me loosened. His arms withdrew, opening, the fingers uncurling, the palms turning upward in a gesture that was simultaneously release and offering. He let me go.

Without a word.

Chapter Twenty

He lifted me off his lap.

The motion was sudden. His hands closed around my waist and rose in one smooth movement. He set me on my feet as if I weighed nothing.

But his hands didn't release.

They stayed at my waist. His fingers pressed through the sheet, firm but not tight. He held on the way people do when they're about to let go, needing the last seconds of contact to remember the shape of me.

Those dark eyes stayed on me. Darker than they'd been in the bone room. Darker than they'd been during the feeding. The gold was receding. His pupils expanded. Behind the familiar hunger, there was something I hadn't seen before.

Fear.

A fear that had nothing to do with prey or predators. A fear of what came next.

He draped the sheet around me. His claws were retracted and careful as they gathered the fabric from my waist. He pulled it over my shoulders and tucked the edges together at my collarbone.

The gesture was so tender that my throat closed around whatever I'd been about to say.

He was covering me. Protecting me. The creature that had torn through this house like a force of nature was handling a cotton sheet as though it could break.

A claw brushed my arm. A single touch. It moved from my shoulder to my elbow and stopped.

Then he stepped back.

One step. Two.

The air between us cooled as his warmth withdrew.

His gaze stayed on me. But it looked distant now. Focused on something behind me, or inside him, something I couldn't see and he couldn't share.

"You have to go."

The words were rasped. Rough. Scraped over the raw inside of a throat that had spoken more tonight than it had in decades. There was urgency beneath the roughness. The urgency of a clock running down.

He moved toward the door of the bone room.

Not to open it for me. To block it.

His body filled the frame. His wings folded tight. His arms hung at his sides. He stood between me and the exit, afraid that if he let me pass, I would turn around. Afraid that if he didn't make me leave now, he would change his mind about letting me go.

I stood in the middle of the room. Bare feet on cold stone. Sheet around my shoulders. Bones above us. Bones below us. Centuries of hunger displayed on every surface.

My pulse was loud in my ears. A steady rhythm that seemed to count down to something.

"Go," he repeated. Softer this time.

The command had lost its edge. Now it sounded closer to a plea. The muscles in his face pulled tight as he fought to hold his resolve. Everything else in him told me to stay. I could see it in his eyes. In his shoulders. In the way his fingers curled and uncurled at his sides.

"What about you?" The words shook out of me, caught between two truths. What had passed between us was real. The blood on the floors above was real too. I stood in the gap between them and couldn't figure out which direction to lean. "You can come with me."

His lips moved. A small motion. Almost a smile, but too sad to become one.

"I can't." The two words fell between us, a door closing.

His eyes held mine. The predatory focus that had defined them all night had dimmed into sorrow.

"I return to the place I came from." He paused. Drew a breath that shuddered on the inhale. "To the dark. Until next time."

The sentence sounded like routine, like this was the shape of his existence.

He came to this world.

He fed.

He went back.

He waited.

He came again.

The pattern made it worse. This was what his life looked like from the inside. Not one night of horror. Endless repetition. Hunger, darkness, satisfaction that faded too fast.

Hell was my word for it.

He had never named the place. The way he spoke of it made names feel too small.

"No." The word left me before I could stop it. "You don't have to." I stepped toward him. My hand found his arm. His skin was warm. The muscle beneath it was taut. "Stay with me." My fingers pressed into him. I felt the pulse under his skin, strong and ancient. "You don't belong there."

His gaze dropped to my hand.

He studied the contact. My fingers on his arm. The pressure of my grip. The warmth passing between us.

His eyes closed.

Slowly.

He held the dark for a moment. He breathed deep. When he opened his eyes again, they were different. Sadder. The gold had dimmed to amber.

"If I stay," he rasped, each word careful, "I won't be able to control myself."

A muscle jumped in his cheek.

"I'll take you with me. To that place." The last two words fractured. "And you..." He swallowed. "You won't like it there."

The truth settled over me, cold and complete.

It wasn't a threat. It wasn't a warning.

It was what he was.

If he stayed, the hunger would return. If the hunger returned, he would lose himself. And if he lost himself while I was near, he wouldn't stop. He would take me back with him into the dark place he came from. Into the nameless dark. Whatever had bloomed between us in this house of death would be swallowed by the hunger that had swallowed everything else.

He was protecting me.

From himself.

The monster that had killed everyone in this house was choosing to send away the one thing he wanted to keep.

"I don't care." My words cracked. They came out smaller than I wanted. "I don't want to lose you."

Claws that could open a human body lifted to my face.

The tip of one traced my cheekbone. It followed the path a tear would take if I'd had any left. The touch was so gentle it barely moved the fine hairs on my skin. The claw continued upward, caught a strand of hair, and guided it behind my ear with careful precision.

"You made me feel something, Rose." The words came rough with effort, each one pulled from somewhere deep. "Something I didn't know I could feel."

His hand lingered at the side of my face. The warmth of his palm spread through me.

"But I won't let you suffer." His thumb brushed my chin. "I won't make you endure that world."

The words left no room to bargain.

I could see the other version of this. The version where I went with him. Where I followed him into the dark. Where I traded everything I was for the chance to keep what we'd found.

I could see it clearly.

He saw that I could see it. The sorrow in his eyes sharpened. He looked like someone watching me reach for a door he would not let me open.

He leaned down.

The kiss was different from every other touch between us. Not the fierce collision in the hallway. Not the hungry claiming of the bedroom.

This was slow.

Deliberate.

His lips moved against mine with a tenderness that made my chest ache. Each press felt like something he couldn't say. Each pull felt like goodbye.

His forehead came to rest against mine.

The contact was warm. Steady. The bones of his skull pressed against mine with soft firmness. His breath mingled with mine, warm and uneven. It carried the taste of milk and salt and something older than either.

"I'll always remember this."

The words were barely louder than his breathing. Intimate. Offered across the small space between our mouths.

I swallowed.

The burn in my throat returned. Words pressed against a passage too tight to let them through. I forced them out.

"I will come back." The words scraped out of me, raw. "I promise."

He pulled back just enough to see my face.

His eyes searched mine. What I saw there was not hope. Not belief. It was acceptance. The look of something that had heard a beautiful promise and did not trust it to survive.

He smiled. It was thin and sad.

Then the smile faded.

What remained was his face. Carved by centuries of hunger and one night of something else. He looked at me with the specific calm of goodbye.

He sighed.

The breath left him slowly. It carried the last of whatever had kept him here, in this moment, at this distance.

I turned away.

The motion took more will than anything else I'd done tonight. More than running. More than fighting. More than pointing at a bed and saying three words.

Turning my back on him felt impossible.

Facing the dark doorway that led up and out of this basement felt impossible.

But I did it. I walked. One foot. Then the other.

The stone floor was cold. My injured foot protested each step. The bandage he'd tied around it held, but it didn't erase the pain. I reached the doorway. The stairs beyond it were dark, rising into the dim light of the hallway above.

I didn't look back.

If I looked back, I wouldn't leave. I knew that with full certainty. One look at him standing in the bone room, surrounded by the evidence of what he was, his eyes gold and his arms empty, would be enough.

I would turn around.

I would go back.

I would stay.

So I climbed.

Step by step.

The wood creaked beneath my weight. The air warmed as I rose. The basement chill gave way to the mansion's stale warmth. I emerged into the hallway and kept moving. My legs carried me by force of will now. Nothing else.

Katie.

I found her in the living room.

She hadn't moved from where the Creeper had tossed her.

She was crumpled on the floor. Her body folded in a way that suggested she'd been dropped rather than placed. Blood from her head wound had spread across the boards beneath her. The stain was larger than it should have been for a wound that size. Her face was slack. Pale. Every muscle had released.

I knelt beside her.

My hands shook as I pressed two fingers against her neck. I pushed through the cool layer of skin to the artery beneath. I held my breath.

Waited.

One second.

Two.

Three.

Then I felt it.

Faint. Distant. But there.

Her heart was still working. Still pushing blood through a body that hadn't given up.

"Katie." My words cracked. "We need to go."

Her eyelids moved. A flutter. Her pupils shifted against the dim light. Her mouth opened, but no sound came out. Her lips were cracked and pale.

She didn't resist. She couldn't.

I hoisted her arm over my shoulder. Her body shifted against mine, dead weight and breath. Her head lolled forward. Her feet dragged as I pulled us both upright.

My muscles screamed. My injured foot sent fire up my ankle and into my calf with every step. Halfway across the room, I felt the bandage give. Wet fabric peeled away from the wound. Blood soaked through. Warm. Slick between my toes.

I made it to the hallway.

Then my legs quit.

My knees hit the floor. Katie came down with me. Her body slid off my shoulder and crumpled beside me on the cold boards. The impact jarred my foot. I bit the inside of my cheek so hard I tasted copper.

For one terrible second, I stayed there.

Hands flat on the floor.

Lungs empty.

The truth formed in my head with cold clarity.

I could not do this.

Katie was too heavy. I was too broken. The door was too far.

This was where it ended.

Then I thought about her face. The way she'd looked at me in the flower shop and said I looked good. The way she'd driven twelve hours without asking why.

I grabbed her under the arms.

I dragged her.

My bare feet slipped in my own blood, and I dragged her anyway. One ugly foot at a time. Down the hallway. Toward the front door.

Every second in this house was a second too many. Every breath of this air was a breath I didn't want to draw. I dragged Katie toward the door with my arm around her waist and her body sagging against mine. The distance between the living room and the front door had been nothing yesterday.

Now it was a marathon measured in feet.

At the door, I paused.

One look.

I'd told myself I wouldn't. I'd told myself looking back would cost more than I could pay. But my body didn't listen to me. It hadn't listened all night.

My head turned.

Just once.

He was there.

He stood in the basement doorway at the far end of the hall. A silhouette against the dark behind him. Wings spread slightly. Shoulders broad. Head tilted in the way I had come to recognize.

The hallway light caught his eyes. Two points of gold in the shadow of his face.

They were fixed on me.

His gaze held too many things. I couldn't separate them. Hunger. Sorrow. Predator. Lover. Goodbye. Promise. All of it layered in the same look.

He looked at me the way you look at something for the last time.

My chest tightened. Sharp. Specific. Deeper than my breastbone. In the place where unsaid things settle and harden.

I turned away.

I pushed the door open.

The October air cut into me, carrying the mineral smell of frost and dead leaves. The sky above was gray, the thin light of early morning pressing through a layer of cloud that covered everything in a flat, cold wash.

The chipped porcelain bowl still sat on the narrow table in the foyer, my keys inside it where I'd dropped them when we arrived. I snatched them up with shaking fingers.

Katie sagged against me as I guided her down the porch steps. Her feet barely lifted. Her weight shifted with each unsteady step.

The gravel was back. The driveway stretched toward the

road as though it had never disappeared. The house had finally let go.

The Honda sat where I'd parked it. Faded blue. Dented bumper. So normal against the horror behind me that my vision blurred, and I had to blink hard to clear it.

I got Katie into the passenger seat. Her head lolled against the window, her breathing shallow but there.

Still there.

I closed her door and went around to the driver's side.

My hands trembled as I slid into the seat. The vinyl was cold. The steering wheel was cold. Everything in the real world was cold in a way that had nothing to do with temperature. It had everything to do with the warmth I'd left behind.

I shoved the key into the ignition and turned it.

The engine caught, coughed, and roared to life with the plain sound of an old machine doing what it was built to do. The vibration traveled through the steering wheel into my hands, up my arms, into my chest, and for a moment I just sat there.

Hands on the wheel.

Engine running.

Looking forward at the driveway that led to the road that led to the highway, the nearest hospital, and whatever came after.

In the rearview mirror, I saw the mansion.

It stood dark and silent against the gray sky. Its cracked stone walls, sagging roof, and shattered windows formed a shape that looked less like a building than a marker. A thing had happened here. Something that would not be forgotten.

Then, from somewhere deep below the house, in the basement, behind the door marked Creatura Noctis, light bloomed.

The symbols carved into the doorframe caught first.

I didn't see it happen, but I knew. After a night like this, some things came through the bones. The carved letters ignited one by one, flame tracing the ancient shapes like a finger down a line of text. The fire started where the magic had been cut into the wood.

Then it ate everything it touched.

It climbed through the basement. Through the floors. It found the old dry timber with absolute certainty. The ground-floor windows glowed orange, then bright, then white. The wood crackled and popped. The sound carried across the still morning air. Smoke began to rise, thin at first, then thick and black against the gray sky.

The roof groaned.

Deep. Structural.

Beams that had held for two centuries finally gave up. A section of the roof collapsed inward and sent sparks into the sky. Then another section fell. Then the east wing vanished into flame so fast it looked less like burning and more like swallowing.

I watched.

The fire ate the mansion in pieces.

The foyer where Sophie had died.

The living room where Brian had sneered and Maya had danced.

The hallway where the Creeper had crawled along the ceiling with his claws tapping a rhythm I would hear in my sleep.

The bedroom where I'd hidden under the bed.

The ballroom where he'd removed the glass from my foot.

The room where he'd called me beautiful and meant it.

The bone room.

Smoke poured from every opening. Every window. Every crack. Every gap in the aging stone. The building burned from the inside out, the fire moving through it with purpose and appetite.

And somewhere inside, inside the smoke, inside the flames, inside the building that was becoming a pyre, the Creeper was there.

Going back.

Returning to the place he came from.

To the dark.

Until next time.

The tears came.

Not many. Not the racking sobs from earlier. Not the steady streams from the bone room.

Just a few.

Hot. Sliding down my cheeks and collecting at my chin.

I didn't wipe them away.

They'd earned the right to fall.

I put the car in gear.

Every press of the pedal sent pain up my leg, but the car moved. The tires crunched on gravel as the Honda rolled forward. Slow at first. Then faster as the driveway met the road and the road stretched ahead, away from the smoke and the fire and the house that had contained the worst and the best of everything I'd ever experienced in a single night.

I didn't look back.

Not at the next intersection. Not at the highway on-ramp. Not at any of the mile markers that passed as the distance between me and Willowcrest grew.

But the rearview mirror was there.

In it, the column of smoke grew smaller with every second. It rose into the morning sky, visible for miles. The crows lifted as one from the iron fence and carried the house's last sight into the morning.

The mansion's final breath.

The last breath of a house that had held its secrets for too long and was finally letting them go.

I drove.

Katie breathed beside me. Still alive.

The road ahead was empty. The October light was pale and real, and the world on the other side of the windshield was the same world I'd left a little over a day ago.

Unchanged by anything that had happened inside those walls.

But I was not the same.

The woman driving this car was not the woman who had driven it here. That woman had carried a cooler of breast milk and a suitcase full of clothes that didn't fit. That woman had planned to confront her former best friend.

That woman was gone.

What remained was someone else. Someone who had seen what humans were capable of and what monsters were capable of. Someone who had learned that the two categories were less separate than she'd been taught.

A part of me was still in that house.

Still in the bone room.

Still in his arms.

Still hearing him say you made me feel something with the rough cadence of a being meeting emotion for the first time.

That part would always be there. It would live in the burned foundation. In the ashes. In whatever remained of

Willowcrest after the fire had taken everything it could reach.

And one thing was certain.

As certain as the road beneath my tires.

As certain as Katie's breath beside me.

As certain as the column of smoke in my mirror that refused to thin or dissolve or disappear.

I was going to keep my promise.

Chapter Twenty-One

ONE YEAR LATER

Halloween had come again. But this time, everything was different.

I stood in the flower shop, trimming the stems of white lilies while afternoon light fell through the front windows and turned the dust motes gold. The air smelled of fresh-cut greenery and damp earth and the faintest thread of rose oil, the scent that had soaked into the walls and the plaster and the worn floorboards over years of arrangements and bouquets.

This shop had become my sanctuary. After Willowcrest, I'd moved south. Katie had moved south six months after me, pretending it was for the job and not because neither of us liked being alone anymore. Maybe grief does that. Pulls you toward the place that nearly killed you, dares you to build something there. Maybe promises do. The original Oklahoma City shop was managed by an assistant I'd hired in the spring. This was the second location, the newest, opened on a corner in the Garden District because the neighborhood reminded me of the kind of place my mama would have liked. Two Rose Gardens across two states. Each one named the same. Each one a marker, a flag planted in the earth that said: *I was here. I survived. I grew.*

"Katie, we're done for the day." I set the shears down and wiped my hands on the apron I'd worn so many times the fabric had thinned at the pockets. My fingers still carried the green smell of stems, the sticky residue of sap.

Katie sat by the window, her hands wrapped around a cup of coffee that had gone lukewarm an hour ago. She wore the same oversized cardigan she'd been wearing since September. The one with the loose threads at the cuffs that she picked at when she was thinking. Her eyes, when they met mine, were soft. Warm. Carrying the gentle, steady concern that had become the baseline of every look she gave me.

She only remembered fragments. Flashes came back without context. The foyer of a house she couldn't picture clearly. A sound she couldn't identify. A feeling of falling. The doctors called it traumatic amnesia, the head wound compounded by smoke inhalation. They said fragments might surface over time, but most of it was gone. Katie didn't fight it. She didn't want those memories back. What little survived the damage she'd buried deep, pressing it down into whatever part of the brain stores the things we're not equipped to face. She didn't ask questions. She didn't push. She accepted the gaps in her memory like a scar, by learning to work around it. Sometimes I caught her watching me, a question almost surfacing in her face.

The others, the police, the investigators, the reporters who'd covered the story for a few weeks before the next disaster gave them fresher grief to feed on. Accepted what I told them. There was a fire. The mansion collapsed while everyone slept. Only Katie and I managed to escape. I'd pulled her from the building. The others — Maya, Brian, Alex, Sophie — hadn't made it out.

The fire had burned too hot for a house that old. By the time investigators reached the lower rooms, there were fragments, not bodies. They blamed structural collapse, animal activity, panic. Nobody looked deeper. Nobody wanted to. The listing vanished before police could trace it. The host account was fake. The payment trail led to a closed prepaid card that had been purchased with cash at a gas station three states away. They wrote their reports. They closed their files. The doctors blamed my foot on broken glass and Katie's head wound on falling debris during the escape. Nobody questioned it. The injuries fit the story.

Only I knew the truth. The whole truth.

"You sure you're okay tonight?" Katie set the mug down, her fingers lingering on the handle. Her brow creased. The old worry line that appeared whenever she was worried about me and trying not to show it. "I don't know... I just have this weird feeling."

It was that time of year. The anniversary. Perhaps she felt it somewhere beneath the damaged memory — not the specifics, not the images — the atmospheric residue of terror, the way a body remembers a trauma the mind has filed away.

"I'll be fine." I forced brightness into my expression, the muscles around my eyes tightening in a pattern I'd practiced until it looked natural. "I've got plans."

Katie didn't push. She never did. After everything we'd been through — the parts she remembered and the parts she didn't — she trusted me enough to let the silence fill in the gaps. She stood, pulled her jacket from the hook by the door, and shrugged into it with the easy, practiced motion of someone who'd done it a thousand times.

"If you need me—"

"I know." My voice softened, the forced brightness giving way to something real. "I'll call."

She smiled like she meant it. The uncomplicated affection of someone who'd been through the worst with you and come out the other side still wanting to sit by your window and drink cold coffee. She held the smile a second longer than necessary, and I could read it: *I see you. I'm here.* Then she turned and walked out into the cool evening. The bell above the door chimed. The sound lingered in the empty shop, ringing itself into silence.

I let out a breath. Stared at the space where she'd been.

After Willowcrest, I stopped waiting for anyone to tell me what I was worth.

Willowcrest did not heal me. It taught me where I still had teeth. The woman who had carried her grief in a cooler and her shame in a scarf cracked open on a ballroom floor, bled through a bandage on a staircase, and dragged her best friend to a car while a mansion burned behind her. What grew back didn't wait for permission.

I stopped apologizing for the space I occupied. Stopped seeing the word *whale* carved into the glass.

I went after Phoenix in court, not out of revenge, or not entirely. Out of the clear, cold recognition that what he'd taken from me during our marriage — my savings, my independence, my self-respect — had a monetary value, and I was owed that value plus interest. The lawsuit peeled back everything he'd kept hidden. The affairs. Maya, and others, a pattern so consistent it was practically a schedule. The financial manipulation. The way he'd systematically dismantled my autonomy so thoroughly that by the time he sent the divorce papers to my hospital bed, I didn't have enough money for a decent attorney.

It took months, more money than I wanted to spend, and three depositions where Phoenix smiled like none of it touched him. But the court saw it all. The evidence was comprehensive. The settlement was generous, generous enough to fund the expansion of The Rose Garden, hire staff, invest in proper equipment, and build the business I'd dreamed of before Phoenix had convinced me that my dreams were smaller than his.

And Phoenix, the man who'd built his entire identity on being adored, on walking into rooms and watching heads turn, on collecting women the way other men collected watches. Lost everything he valued.

Slowly, the way rot works. The settlement went public, and with it the affairs, and the social circle that had orbited him, planets around a sun, discovered that the sun was, in fact, a black hole. Business partners distanced themselves. The invitations stopped arriving. The women who had lined up for his attention, who had laughed at his jokes and tolerated his arrogance because the package it came in was expensive, vanished the moment the package lost its wrapping.

Last I heard, he was working a mid-level position at a firm that had never heard of him, living in a one-bedroom apartment in a part of the city where nobody cared what car you drove or who you used to be. The man who had thrown me away because I didn't fit the life he'd been building for an audience was now living a life so unremarkable that nobody would bother to polish it. He wasn't ruined. He wasn't destroyed. He was something worse.

He was irrelevant. Invisible. The thing he had made me feel for years — unseen, unimportant, not worth the effort of looking at — had become the defining quality of his own existence. Nobody's first choice. Nobody's choice at all.

I pushed the thought aside. I wasn't the woman who dwelled on Phoenix anymore. He occupied the same mental space as a bill I'd already paid, filed, finished, the balance at zero.

I locked up the shop. The deadbolt turned with a solid, satisfying click that echoed in the empty street. My car, a newer one now, not the dented Honda, a modest sedan that started on the first turn and didn't smell like the past, sat at the curb. I drove home through streets that were already showing signs of the evening to come. Pumpkins on stoops. Fake cobwebs stretched across porch railings. A skeleton propped in a lawn chair outside a bar, a beer bottle wired into its bony hand.

Halloween. The night the world dressed up as monsters and called it fun.

Chapter Twenty-Two

Inside the apartment, the scent of pumpkin spice greeted me. I'd made it a ritual. Lighting the candles every evening when I got home, letting sugar and wax saturate the rooms so that coming home felt like arriving rather than returning. The apartment was different now. No longer the cold, unfamiliar space I'd moved into after the divorce. I'd made it mine. The walls held photographs. The shelves held books. The kitchen counter held evidence of a life being lived, a fruit bowl, a stack of mail, a candle that had burned down to a nub and needed replacing.

But some things hadn't changed.

The old pull came as I hung up my jacket, the pressure building behind the tissue, the reminder that my body was still operating a function that had no recipient. The milk still came. Less than before, the volume had tapered, the nightly sessions with the pump shorter, the ache less urgent. But it hadn't stopped. Every morning, every evening, the rhythm hadn't changed, only the reason. My body, in its stubborn, biological persistence, continued to produce what it had been producing since the pregnancy that ended on a kitchen floor, as though the machinery didn't care that the product had no destination.

I still donated. Every week, the cooler went to the milk bank, filled from my morning and evening sessions. I told myself it was because good had to come from the nightmare. That if my body insisted on this function, the least I could do was direct it toward someone who needed it. A baby some- where, faceless and unnamed, drinking what my baby never could.

But that was only the clean version. And tonight, on this night of all nights, I could admit the rest to myself.

I kept producing because he was coming back.

I didn't know it the way you know a fact, with evidence, certainty, with the rational confidence of a conclusion supported by data. I knew it the way you know the season is about to change, a shift in the air, a quality of light, an atmos- pheric signal that arrives before the event itself. He was coming. I could feel it. The way I'd felt the pressure change in the mansion before his wings were audible. The way I'd felt his presence under the bed before I turned my head.

He was close.

I changed quickly. The black dress hung in the closet where I'd placed it a week ago, long sleeves, simple cut, the fabric falling straight from the shoulders to just below the knee. I pulled it on. The material was soft against my skin, and as I fastened the buttons, my fingers brushed my breast.

The touch was light. Accidental. But the contact sent a cascade of memory through me before thought could catch up. My hands stopped and my breath caught and for three full seconds I was back in the bone room, his mouth on me, his arms around me, his voice saying *why would you do this for a monster like me* with the rough, broken cadence of a creature encountering grace for the first time.

I finished the buttons. My hands were shaking, not from fear.

The witch's hat sat on the dresser. I picked it up and set it on my head, adjusting the angle in the mirror. The reflection that looked back at me was someone I was still getting to know. A woman with dark hair and brown eyes and a body that was soft and round and strong, wearing a black dress that fit because she'd bought it in her actual size instead of the size she wished she was. The woman in the mirror didn't flinch. Didn't adjust her posture to minimize. Didn't drape a scarf over her chest.

The woman in the mirror looked ready.

I reached for my keys.

The doorbell rang.

My hand froze over the key ring. The sound wasn't the cheerful, rapid-fire burst of trick-or-treaters, the staccato knocking of small fists, the giggling, the rehearsed chorus of *trick or treat*. This was a single press. Sustained. Deliberate. The sound of someone who knew exactly who was on the other side of the door and was announcing themselves with the confidence of someone expected.

I crossed the room. My heels clicked across the hardwood, each step a controlled effort to keep my legs from shaking. The door was solid wood, painted white, fitted with a peephole I didn't use. I didn't need to. I could feel him on the other side like a fire through a wall, there in the warmth on my palm by the warmth on your palm.

I opened the door.

He was there.

Tall. The height was the same, enough to make doorframes look undersized and ceilings feel lower. But the rest was different. The wings were gone. The grayish-green, veined skin was gone. The claws, the angular planes, the predatory geometry of the face I'd kissed in a blood-soaked hallway. All of it was gone, replaced by something that looked human. Looked. The word was important. He looked human the way a wolf can pass for a dog, the shape was right, the proportions were plausible, but something behind the eyes gave the lie to the disguise.

His features were sharp. Jaw defined, cheekbones high, a face that people notice and then can't stop noticing, that draws the eye and holds it with a force that has nothing to do with conventional attractiveness and everything to do with presence. His eyes, and this was where the disguise thinned, where the human costume frayed at the seams, were dark. Too dark. The irises were so deep they swallowed the light that hit them, returning nothing, reflecting nothing, two pools of concentrated attention that locked onto mine the moment the door opened.

A slow smile spread across his face, nothing like the wide, tooth-baring grin of the Creeper. Softer. A lifting of the corners, a softening of the jaw, an expression that managed to be both familiar and utterly new.

"Can I help you?" The words left me in a whisper. My hand gripped the edge of the door, my knuckles blanching against the painted wood.

He stepped inside. Through the space I occupied, his body displacing mine, his presence filling the apartment as it had filled every room he'd ever entered. He didn't wait for an invitation. He didn't need one. His eyes stayed on mine as he moved, and the air between us shifted with the electricity of two bodies that have shared something that neither of them has shared with anyone else.

"You don't recognize me yet?" His voice was different in this form. Smoother. The grinding, subterranean resonance was gone, replaced by something that sounded almost human, a low baritone, slightly rough at the edges, carrying an accent that belonged to no country and every century. But beneath the surface polish, I could hear it, the same voice. The same weight behind the words. The same attention directed at the same person.

I blinked. The disconnect between what I was seeing and what I was feeling created a kind of vertigo, the human face, the human body, the human clothes, set against the unmistakable, bone-deep recognition that the thing inside the disguise was the thing that had crawled across a ceiling and wept in a bone room and pressed its forehead against my chest and whispered *chosen*.

His gaze dropped to my chest. His lips parted. Slightly, involuntarily, the reflex of a mouth that remembered what it had tasted. The motion was small but I caught it, and the catching sent a jolt through me that started at my sternum and radiated outward, and the memories came, not one at a time but all at once, a flood, every sensation from that night compressed into a single instant of recognition.

The ballroom. The bone room. His mouth on me. His arms around me. The fire in the rearview mirror.

"How?" I stepped back, my hands finding the kitchen counter behind me, needing something solid. "How are you here?"

His smile deepened with the same patience he'd used in

the mansion, the patience of a creature with time and no reason to rush. He stepped closer, and the distance between us shrank from feet to inches, and I could feel the heat radiating from his body, different in this form, less intense, but unmistakably his.

"I came out because of you." The words were soft. Intimate. Delivered at a volume meant for one person in one room. "This shape holds. I chose it. The same way you chose me."

I stared. Tried to reconcile the human face with the creature I'd known. Tried to map the angles of the one onto the other, to find the correspondences, to prove to myself that the recognition I felt was justified by evidence and not just by the desperate hope of a woman who'd been waiting for a knock at her door.

"But you were—"

"Different." He finished the sentence for me, his voice shifting, dropping a register, the surface smoothness giving way to a darker sound that rumbled low and reminded me of stone walls, flickering lights, and iron. "Yes. I was." A pause. His eyes held mine with an intensity that made the air between us feel solid. "But you... you pulled me back, Rose. You're the reason I returned to this world." The darkness in his voice deepened. "Do you even know what you've done to me? What I've been craving all this time?"

My pulse was a drum in my ears. His proximity pressed against me. Atmospheric, a storm against a window before it breaks. Every nerve in my body was firing, every sense straining toward him, every cell participating in the recognition that the thing I'd been waiting for was standing three feet away in a human suit.

He stepped closer. The final step. The one that eliminated

the distance entirely. His breath was warm on my forehead, my cheeks, my lips.

"The dark clawed at me." His voice was low. Strained. Each word sounded forced through stone. "Everything was chaos." His eyes searched my face. Moving from my eyes to my mouth to the curve of my jaw and back, rapid, hungry, a hand reaching for something it had been denied. "But through it all, there was one thing that kept me going."

My body tightened. Everything inside me contracting, pulling inward, bracing for the impact of whatever he was about to say.

"The dark had your name in it."

The words came out jagged. Rough. Each one torn from a place that resisted giving them up. They didn't sound like a declaration. They sounded like a confession. The admission of something that had been eating at him from the inside, growing in the dark, demanding release.

"I did not know humans called that love. But I have carried it since that night." His throat tightened between sentences, the effort bunching the muscles there, the effort of speaking visible in every line of his face. "I've seen you in every shadow." His hand rose toward me — trembling, the fingers not quite steady — and stopped just short of my cheek, hovering, as if the act of touching me required permission he wasn't sure he'd been granted. "Tasted you in every breath."

A hand found my cheek. The contact was warm. Human-warm, not Creeper-warm. Heat pulsed beneath the skin.

"I have wanted you in ways your language cannot hold."

His need hit me like weather. This was not cautious human love. It was feral. Desperate. The nameless dark had not thinned it.

"You've haunted me," he breathed. The word *haunted* carried an irony neither of us acknowledged. "You're the only thing that made sense in all that madness." His thumb moved across my cheekbone, a slow, sweeping stroke, tracing the geography of my face. "And now that I'm here..." His voice dropped to a whisper. The sound was barely more than shaped breath. "I'm never letting you go."

I surged forward.

My hands found the front of his shirt and pulled, closing the distance in one violent motion. My mouth hit his. This kiss held everything the farewell kiss hadn't, a year of missing and hunger. His lips were warmer in this form. Smoother. But the need behind them was the same, a low growl moving from his chest into mine, his mouth reclaiming territory it had mapped once before.

"I love you too." The words fell out between breaths, between kisses, spilling from my mouth into his. I didn't plan them. Didn't rehearse them. They had been waiting under my tongue for a year. "I mean it."

He pulled back, barely an inch. His forehead rested against mine. His breath was ragged, his body trembling with the effort of restraint.

"You made me feel alive, Rose." The roughness was back in his voice, the gravel, the depth, the echo of a voice older than any country speaking through a human mouth. "Made me want to be something more than darkness."

I pulled back far enough to see his face. My fingers traced the lines of his jaw, his cheekbones, the architecture of a face that was new and old at the same time. My chest was full, a year of want finally finding a place to go.

"What now?" I asked. The question was soft. Open.

Carrying no expectation, no demand. Just curiosity. The honest curiosity of a woman standing in her kitchen with a monster-turned-man on Halloween night, wondering what comes next.

A deep chuckle rumbled through him, the sound traveling from his chest into the air between us, warm and low. His head tilted, the motion birdlike, familiar, a gesture that belonged to his other form and had carried over into this one.

"You tell me." His dark eyes crinkled at the corners. "What do humans do on Halloween?"

I bit back a smile. "They dress up. Pretend to be someone else for the night."

His eyes narrowed, a flicker of confusion crossing the human features, the Creeper's intelligence working through an unfamiliar concept. "I am pretending to be someone else." He looked down at his human body, his hands turning palm-up, examining them. "Does that count?"

"I guess for tonight you can be yourself." My fingers moved to the top button of my dress. The button slipped through the fabric, and then the next one, and the collar parted, and the cool air of the apartment touched the skin of my chest. "Lose the human form." My eyes held his. "It's Halloween. No one will question it."

Understanding dawned. I watched it move across his face, the realization arriving in stages, first as comprehension, then as wonder, then as a grin that spread slowly and widely and held. The grin belonged entirely to the Creeper. Too wide, too knowing, carrying the amusement of an ancient thing handed a gift it didn't expect.

"They'll think I'm one of them." The grin widened.

"Exactly." I felt the corners of my own mouth lifting. "You don't have to hide. Not tonight."

In one fluid motion — a ripple, a shift, the human skin peeling back like a costume being shed — he changed. The transformation was seamless. The tall, sharp-featured man dissolved, and in his place stood the creature I knew. The dark wings unfurled behind him, stretching to fill the kitchen, the membranes catching the candlelight. His skin was grayish-green, veined with black, the muscles visible beneath the surface. His eyes burned gold.

He looked at me. I looked back. Neither of us flinched.

Together, we stepped into the cool Halloween night.

The streets buzzed with life. Costumes everywhere, vampires and witches and zombies and things that had no name, all moving through the evening in a river of color and noise. Music drifted from open doorways. Children ran ahead of their parents, plastic pumpkins swinging from their fists, their laughter bright and careless in the dark air.

He walked beside me. His wings were folded tight against his back, his stride adjusted to match mine, his gold eyes sweeping the crowd with an alertness that never fully relaxed. Looking at him, people's minds translated terror into costume before fear could fully form. People looked at him. Of course they looked. He stood a head above the tallest person in the street, and his appearance, the wings, the veins, the grayish-green skin veined with black, the eyes that glowed in the streetlight, demanded attention.

But it was Halloween.

"Great costume, man!" A teenager in a hockey mask gave him a thumbs-up as he passed.

"Dude, that's insane. Where'd you get the wings?" A man in a pirate hat stopped to stare, his girlfriend pulling him along.

"You look amazing!" A group of women in matching cat

ears clustered around him, phones out, asking for photos. He stood still while they posed beside him, their screens angled for selfies. Later, when they checked their cameras, every shot of him would be the same. A smear of shadow and wings where a face should have been, the image refusing to resolve no matter how many times they tapped the screen. But they wouldn't remember that. They'd remember the costume. The compliment. The thrill of standing next to a thrill they couldn't quite place.

He stood stiffly among them, jaw tight each time someone came too close. I could see the flicker of unease in his expression, the brief tension in his hands as he resisted instincts that had served him for centuries. But the compliments kept coming, and the smiles were genuine, and nobody screamed, and nobody ran, and slowly — degree by degree, like ice warming in a palm — the tension in his body eased.

I adjusted my witch's hat, the cheap pointed tip wobbling in the breeze. My heels clicked against the pavement, and with each step the pressure in my feet increased, the straps digging into my ankles, the balls of my feet aching, the accumulating discomfort of walking farther than the shoes were designed for. I shifted my weight, trying to redistribute the pain, and my pace slowed without my permission.

He noticed before I'd finished the thought.

His arms were around me before I could protest, one beneath my knees, one behind my back, the motion so smooth and effortless that my feet left the ground in the same second that my brain registered his intention. He cradled me against his chest, my body settling into his arms as though the space had been designed for me, his grip and my body calibrated to fit.

"I'm heavy," I murmured. The words were reflexive, the same words I'd been saying my entire adult life, the automatic disclaimer that preceded any situation in which my body's weight became someone else's responsibility. The phrase carried the ghost of every comment, every look, every measured pause that had taught me to apologize for the space I occupied.

The gold in his eyes stayed warm. Not burning. Not flaring. Steady, with the certainty of a creature that saw clearly and was not disappointed. The lips curved into a small, certain smile that carried the authority of a being that had held me before and would hold me again and found the holding to be the opposite of a burden.

"No, you're not." The words were firm. Final. Delivered with the same unshakeable certainty he'd used in the bone room when he'd said *this is what I am.* He wasn't arguing. He wasn't reassuring. He was correcting an error. Stating a fact. Replacing false information with true.

"You're perfect."

My chest ached with the fullness of being seen by a creature with no reason to flatter me, no social script to follow, no human reason to lie. He carried me through the Halloween crowd as if I weighed nothing, and the nothing wasn't a comment on my body. It was a comment on his strength, on the effortlessness of holding what he loved.

We walked until the crowd thinned and my feet ached and the night had done what it was supposed to do, given us a window, a sliver of normal, a few hours of walking through the world together without the world burning down around us. Then I led him back.

Epilogue

The flower shop was dark when we arrived. I unlocked the door — the deadbolt turning with that same solid click — and we stepped inside. The bell chimed once above us, then fell silent. The air was cool and smelled of roses and damp earth and the green-water scent of stems sitting in their overnight buckets. I locked the door behind us.

This was my place. My ground. The shop I'd built from the wreckage of everything that had been taken from me. And he was here, inside it, his wings brushing the displays as he moved through the narrow aisle, his gold eyes taking in the flowers. The colors, the textures, the impossible delicacy of petals, with the focused attention of a predator encountering beauty it had no framework for.

He set me down on the old stool behind the counter. The wood was cool. His hands lingered at my waist, fingers pressing gently against the fabric of my dress, a second too long, the touch of someone who doesn't want to stop touching.

My pulse steadied. I knew what was coming, and this time I stayed present for it.

I reached for the buttons of my dress. My fingers worked them slowly — one, then the next, then the next — the fabric parting to reveal the skin beneath, the curves that he had studied in a ballroom, that he had worshipped in a bone room, that he had chosen in a voice that had never lied. The cool shop air touched my bare chest, and the sensation was different from every other time I'd been exposed. Present. Open. Mine to give.

His gaze darkened. The familiar hunger was there. It would always be there, structural, inseparable from what he was. But layered over it, visible in the softening of his brow and the slight parting of his lips, was the other thing. The thing that had made him weep. The thing that had brought him back from the dark.

He knelt before me.

He lowered himself between the flower buckets, wings settling as his hands came to rest on my waist. The same posture from the bone room, but different now. There was no bargain now, no blood on the floor, and no one left to save. Just two beings who had found each other, choosing to be here, surrounded by roses.

The gaze traced my face the way you read a letter you've waited for. Warm hands on my waist. Steady. Trembling only slightly.

The moment his lips touched my chest, every nerve in my body ignited. His kiss was slow, tracing a path from my collarbone to the curve of my breast, and I shivered beneath the attention, my fingers finding his hair, threading into it, curling against his scalp.

Then a low sound moved through my ribcage before I heard it in the air, and he began to drink.

His feeding was measured. Each pull came with care, nothing like the sharp pleasure of the mansion. This was quieter. Warmer. The intimacy of being needed by something that had never been given to freely. My fingers tightened in his hair and I pressed him closer, and the shop around us — the flowers, the counter, the bell above the door — faded until there was nothing but this. His mouth on me. My body sustaining him. The oldest rhythm in the world, playing out in a flower shop on the one night of the year when monsters walk among humans and nobody looks twice.

When he finally pulled away, his eyes were glossy. Raw. Grief and joy and hunger and love, nothing in his face knew how to hide, the whole helpless flood of a being that had existed for centuries without tenderness suddenly drowning in it.

His chest rose and fell with deep, shuddering breaths. His wet lips trembled. He looked up at me from his knees, and the expression on his face was the expression of someone who has been given something they don't know how to hold.

"I came out of the dark," he whispered. The words were thick. Heavy. Carrying the gravity of a truth finally allowed into the air. "For you." His hands tightened on my waist without hurting me, the grip of a creature that had found the one anchor keeping it from being pulled back into the dark. "No one had ever given me anything. Not willingly. It changed the door. It changed the hunger." His throat worked, the muscles bunching. "Near you, the hunger quiets. Away from you, it still screams. What you give me is enough to keep me here. It does not make me harmless. But here — with you

— I can stay, Rose." His eyes searched mine. "If you want me to."

Tears. Mine this time. They welled from a place I'd thought I'd emptied, a reservoir I'd been drawing from all year, for the grief and the healing and the rebuilding, that turned out to have one more layer. One more pocket of emotion, held in reserve for this exact moment. They blurred my vision, softened the gold of his eyes into a warm, shimmering light.

My hand found his cheek. The skin was rough. The warmth beneath it pulsed. My thumb traced the line of his cheekbone. The same path his claw had traced across mine on the night we'd met, when he'd wiped a tear from my face with a touch so gentle it had opened a sealed place in my chest that had never fully closed.

"I want you," I breathed. The words came out skinned. Exposed. Carrying no armor, no qualification, no fine print. "Stay."

He kissed me.

The contact was soft. Reverent. His lips against mine with a pressure that was barely there. The ghost of a touch, the suggestion of a kiss, as though the fullness of what he felt could only be expressed at the lightest possible volume. His hands moved from my waist to my face, cupping my jaw, holding me carefully, as though surprise itself had weight.

The kiss ended. I sat on that stool in my flower shop with his forehead against mine and his hands on my face, and I knew this was real. The woman who had driven to a haunted mansion with a cooler of breast milk and a heart full of grief had built a life from the ruins. The edges didn't match. The seams showed. The shape of the life I'd assembled was irreg-

ular and strange and built on a foundation that included a creature from a realm that had no name. But it held. And it was
mine.

And in his arms, in the flower shop that smelled of roses
and earth, with Halloween leaking through the locked door and
his steady gold eyes on mine, I stayed.

Also by Sephyrra

The Primal Sins Collection

A series of dark horror romances. Each book a standalone. Each monster ruined for one woman, and one woman only.

Insatiable — The Primal Sins Collection Book 1

She went to the Halloween party already broken — by the husband who left and the friend who helped him do it. She wasn't looking for trouble. But a monster who feeds on fear caught her scent, and on her, he smelled something else. Something he'd been waiting a long time to taste.

Drenched — The Primal Sins Collection Book 2

She came to the fog-locked village for the ocean's secrets. The ocean had been keeping one for her — something old, something patient, something that had been hearing her name in the tide for years before she ever arrived.

Devoured — The Primal Sins Collection Book 3

St. Dymphna's locks women like her away. The ones who killed their husbands. The ones nobody wants to remember. Six hundred years the Executioner has paced the asylum floor. He carved the grooves himself. He was made to kill her. He didn't.

Touched — The Primal Sins Collection Book 4

She married a man who controls everything she does. She moved into his first wife's house. And in the attic, behind dust and silence, something that has watched her longer than she knows finally found its way through the glass.

Once Upon a Monster

Dark fairy tale retellings with mature curvy heroines.

Claiming Red — Once Upon a Monster Book 1

They called her Red for the cloak she wore. Soon they'd call her Red for the blood she spilled. She ran into the forest that swallowed six armed men and sent back pieces. Something was waiting in her dead grandmother's cottage. He watched her like he'd been starving his whole life — and he had.

Bride of the Haunted Manor

A standalone gothic romance novella.

She took the caretaker job at Blackwood Manor because she needed a fresh start. Thirty-eight years of pain will do that. Her gift lets her speak to spirits, and the manor has plenty. But one of them isn't just haunting the halls — he's haunting her. A love that crosses the line between the living and the dead, and a sinister force buried in the walls that wants to claim them both.

Acknowledgments

To my fellow indie dark romance authors—you know who you are. You're the ones who understand that a little darkness never hurt anyone (except maybe our characters). Keep writing those morally questionable heroes and making the rest of us look sane by comparison.

To my husband: Your tolerance for my disappearing acts into the writing cave is legendary. I don't know how you manage it, but I'm grateful. You've been my anchor through the chaos, and yes, you're probably the only one who could put up with my process. Gold star for you.

Sonia, my sister—this is big. You read my book. And you *liked* it. I've got to say, that's a high compliment. I've written plenty of things, but hearing you say it was good? That felt like a win. Thanks for being my first reader and not being horrified by what goes on in my head.

About the Author

Sephyrra writes from the shadows where horror and desire collide.

Mother, wife, writer, unrepentant procrastinator — usually all at once, rarely in that order. She believes the best monsters are the ones we invite in, and the most interesting heroines are plus-size, over 35, and deliciously damaged.

Author of the Primal Sins series and the Once Upon a Monster dark fairy tale retellings, she splits her time between novels, scripts, and staring at blank pages while pretending to work. Writing isn't just her life — it's her obsession, her therapy, and probably the reason her family eats so much takeout.

instagram.com/Authorsephyrra
facebook.com/Authorsephyrra

Author's Note

I've always had a thing for horror, creatures, and monsters—
call it teratophilia if you must. When I first watched *Jeepers
Creepers* as a teen, I wasn't horrified by the Creeper... I was
intrigued. And well, that fascination is pretty much what led to
this book.

A Note of Thanks

Dear Reader,

Thank you from the bottom of my heart for diving into this story and making it all the way to the end. Your time and imagination are truly valued, and I hope you enjoyed Rose's story as much as I loved bringing it to life.

If you'd like to help indie authors like myself, here are a few ways you can make a big impact:

1. Leave a Review:

Your honest review means the world! Even a few sentences on Amazon, Goodreads, or wherever you purchased the book can help more readers discover new stories.

2. Spread the Word:

Tell your friends, family, or fellow book lovers about this book! Word of mouth is one of the best ways to help indie books find new readers.

3. Follow on Social Media:

Stay connected! Follow me on social media @authorse-phyrra to stay updated on upcoming releases, behind-the-scenes content, and more. Every follow and share helps grow this amazing community.

Thank you again for your support. Indie authors thrive because of readers like you, and I can't wait to share more stories with you in the future!

With gratitude,

Sephyrra